# OLIVE JONES and the MEMORY THIEF

## KATE GILBY SMITH

Orion

ORION CHILDREN'S BOOKS

First published in Great Britain in 2022
by Hodder & Stoughton

3 5 7 9 10 8 6 4

A CIP catalogue record for this book is available from the British Library.

ISBN 978 1 51010 852 3

Typeset in Sabon by Avon DataSet Ltd, Alcester, Warwickshire

Printed and bound in Great Britain by Clays Ltd, Elcograf S.p.A.

The paper and board used in this book are made from
wood from responsible sources.

Orion Children's Books
An imprint of
Hachette Children's Group
Part of Hodder & Stoughton
Carmelite House
50 Victoria Embankment
London EC4Y 0DZ

An Hachette UK Company
www.hachette.co.uk
www.hachettechildrens.co.uk

For my grandparents

# CONTENTS

# CHAPTER ONE

# The Funeral of Grandma Sylvie

Olive Jones was looking through her bedroom window at the bungalow opposite. For almost thirteen years – in other words, Olive's entire life – her grandmother had lived just across the road. And now the house was empty.

Those who'd attended the funeral service had been invited to Olive's home afterwards for a hastily arranged buffet and cups of tea. Olive had filled her pockets with cheese sandwiches and escaped to her bedroom as quickly as she could. She'd wanted desperately to be away from all the gloom.

Truth be told, in that moment Olive found being gloomy quite difficult. It wasn't that she didn't feel sad that her grandmother had passed away. It was just that, well, she hadn't really *known* her. Their houses were barely twenty metres apart. And yet Grandma Sylvie might as well have lived in another country. Though she'd retired from her job as an accountant years before they were born, somehow she'd always been too busy to pop over to visit her grandchildren. On birthdays she used to drop cards through the letterbox for Olive and her younger brother Frankie with crisp ten-pound notes tucked inside. By the time the card reached the doormat, however, no matter how fast the children got to the door, she was nowhere to be seen. She'd always been invited for Christmas but hadn't ever shown up. Sometimes months would go by without a single sighting of her. Whenever Olive *had* encountered her grandmother – passing her on the pavement, say – the elderly lady would smile and then quickly rush away before Olive could do more than open her mouth. On these occasions, Olive often had a feeling there was something Grandma Sylvie wanted to say, but after years passed without her grandmother ever breaking her silence, Olive decided this was only wishful thinking.

Even so, Olive had learned a little about her grandmother over the years. Olive knew that she liked to keep informed about world events; Grandma Sylvie collected the newspaper from her doorstep first thing every morning. Olive could tell that she cared about helping wildlife, having seen how she faithfully restocked the birdfeeder in her front garden, sometimes feeding the robins straight from her hand. Olive also knew that her grandmother was exceptionally fit. On a few occasions, Olive had seen her sprinting around the block after dark. Twice she'd witnessed her using a thick tree branch for a round of pull-ups. And once Olive had seen her grandmother trip over a garden hose and turn the fall into a perfect somersault, landing firmly on both feet and walking away without even a pause. As remarkable as those occurrences were, Olive felt certain she was the only person to have noticed them. Nobody else was paying attention. In the eyes of her neighbours, Sylvie Jones was simply an elderly woman who preferred to keep to herself.

When she was younger, Olive had secretly wished for a replacement grandmother. She wanted the kind of grandmother she'd heard about. The kind some of her friends at school were lucky enough to have, the ones who liked things such as gardening and watching daytime murder-mysteries. The type who pinched cheeks and produced endless pear drops from their handbags. She would have liked a grandmother who read bedtime stories. The very thought of

Grandma Sylvie doing any of these things was frankly preposterous.

'She's just old fashioned,' explained Olive's mother. 'She doesn't like to make a fuss.'

But Olive was far from satisfied by this explanation. As she got older, she stopped wishing for a new grandmother and instead became intensely interested in the one she had. *Why is Grandma Sylvie so secretive?* she wondered. *What keeps her so busy all the time? Why does she stay so fit and strong? What if . . . she's hiding something?*

Olive's mother had found this suggestion quite amusing. 'What on earth do you think a lady in her eighties might be hiding?' she'd said. 'Your grandmother worked hard as an accountant and these days she likes to take advantage of her well-earned retirement to travel and stay active. Exercise helps her arthritis.'

But Olive wasn't convinced. There had to be more to it. 'Maybe she likes to travel. *Or . . .* maybe she has a secret life she doesn't want us to find out about!' she'd replied.

Olive's mother laughed even louder. 'Sorry to disappoint you, Olive. We're not the kind of family who has secrets. What you see is what you get.

You have an overactive imagination.'

*What you see is what you get.* Well, if you asked Olive, what she saw of her grandmother was decidedly strange. As for having an overactive imagination, Olive couldn't deny *that* was true.

The thing was, Olive wanted desperately for her life to be more exciting than it actually was. She wanted it to be more like the films and TV shows she loved to watch, with their explosions and car chases and daring rescues. If you asked her to, she could recite lines from at least twenty-seven different films by heart. Olive herself, however, was nothing like the heroes of her favourite action movies. She was tall for her age, with long dark hair that annoyed her if it wasn't tucked behind her ears, and she had a slightly pointier chin than most. She was also the third fastest runner in her entire year group, thanks to her very long legs. But by all other measures, Olive was distinctly average. With the exception, of course, of her imagination.

Olive was a world-class dreamer – growing up in a place where *nothing ever happens* will do that to a person. Any perfectly innocent creak of a floorboard was always, in Olive's mind, something much more dramatic – a gang of thieves searching for hidden valuables or a pack of vampires hunting for their latest snack. If she heard a car engine backfire when out walking with her mother and brother, Olive's mind would race straight to bank robberies and diamond heists. One time, she'd been utterly convinced that the local postman was lacing letters with poison as revenge for being chased by neighbourhood dogs. He had been quite surprised on his morning rounds to find her spying on him from the bushes. Then there was the supply teacher at school, Mr Harold, who Olive had suspected of being an escaped high-security prisoner she'd seen on the morning news. Mr Harold hadn't been too happy when Olive had confronted him about it. (In her defence, they did have very similar-looking sideburns.)

Olive's imagination was always getting her into trouble. Her school report was littered with descriptions such as 'must try harder to concentrate' or 'can't seem to settle in class' or 'often distracts her classmates'. Olive wanted to do better – she really did – but somehow, she couldn't help going that little bit too far. She was the one who set fire to her lab coat in science the very first time they were allowed to use Bunsen burners. The one who tried to climb the oak tree in the playground and got stuck halfway up, so the fire brigade had to be called to get her down. The one who *accidentally* started a rebellion when the teachers tried to ban unhealthy food at lunchtime (but to be fair to Olive, how could she have possibly predicted that her speech defending pizza would cause a food fight?).

Her biggest problem was, as much as she tried to listen to her teachers in class, Olive could never stop her mind from wandering. It didn't help that Olive's brother, Frankie, who was two years younger, was a model student. Like his sister, Frankie was tall for his age, with a head of dark brown hair that fell over his eyes. Unlike his sister, Frankie was often described as 'a shy but thoughtful student' by his teachers (and a 'swot' or a 'geek' by his less-kind classmates). People were always surprised to find out who his sister was. Olive was sometimes surprised they were related too. Frankie was a proud member of both the choir and orchestra, as well as captain of the chess club, activities which kept him late after school most afternoons. (Olive often stayed late too, but in her case it was for detention rather than extra-curricular activities.) Though they'd been thick as thieves when they were younger, they rarely spent much time together these days. She'd never admit it, but Olive was a little jealous of her brother. Why couldn't she be more like him? Why couldn't she learn to behave herself?

Still – as far as Olive was concerned – just because *sometimes* she got carried away with her imagination, and *some* of her previous theories about people in the neighbourhood had missed the mark, it didn't mean that she wasn't right about Grandma Sylvie.

She just couldn't shake the feeling that there was more to her grandmother's life than she was letting on. So, for a long time, Olive held on tightly to her suspicions, perhaps because the alternative – that her grandmother didn't *want* to get to know her – was too sad a thought to accept.

It was only when Grandma Sylvie passed away from a suspected heart attack, aged eighty-four, that Olive decided the time had come to let her suspicions go. Her mother was clearly right. Olive had let herself get carried away again. There were no secrets to discover – only a grandmother she had never really known. And one that now she never would.

This realisation had stayed with Olive for the duration of the funeral, and on the ride back to their house afterwards in the long black car, and as relatives crowded into their living room and started helping themselves to pineapple on sticks. And it was all she was thinking about now, sitting on her bed, watching her grandmother's house across the road.

The bungalow itself was perfectly ordinary looking, with grey, pebble-dashed walls and white lace curtains that were always kept closed. The garden at the front was overgrown with a flaky wooden gate that swung creakily in the wind. The house felt – like Olive's relationship with its former inhabitant – both completely familiar and utterly mysterious.

Olive again wished, as she had done many times before, that she could peel back the bungalow's lace curtains and take a look inside. What would she find there? She knew she would have to go back to the buffet in the living room soon – she'd already heard her mother call her name more than once – but she gave herself a few more minutes to take it in.

Olive tried to memorise her grandmother's house. It would be sold soon, and no doubt the new occupant would change things. They'd fix the gate, and replace the old-fashioned curtains, and weed the garden, and in so doing, take away all the things Olive had grown to like about the place over the years.

She was squinting, imagining how the bungalow would look with all those changes, when something caught her eye.

A twitch of white lace.

Olive blinked, straightening up. At first, she thought her eyes must have been playing tricks on her. It had been a long morning, after all, and she'd probably eaten one too many pocketed cheese sandwiches.

Then it happened again. This time it was clear. One of the lace curtains had moved. No, it hadn't moved. Curtains don't twitch on their own accord, or not usually anyway. One of the lace curtains had *been* moved.

Somebody was in the house, Olive realised with a start. But that couldn't be. Her mother had the only key and Olive could still hear her talking in the other room. The house should have been empty.

*Who could be in there?* she wondered, and as she thought it, a hand appeared as if from nowhere and drew the curtains aside. Olive gasped. She uncrossed her legs and rose on to her knees. Her face was so close to the window now that her breath fogged up the glass. The truth was undeniable. Somebody was standing at the window of her grandmother's house. Not only that, but they were *looking directly at her.*

It had never occurred to Olive, in all the time she'd watched her grandmother's house, that *she* could also be watched. She jumped backwards, half falling off the bed.

Olive took a breath to calm her racing heart, and then, slowly, she returned to her place at the window. The person standing in Grandma Sylvie's house raised their hand and waved. It wasn't a wave of greeting, although that would have been strange enough.

It was, unmistakably, a wave which said . . . *come here*.

# CHAPTER TWO

# An Unexpected Inheritance

Even for those who spend their entire lives wishing for out-of-the-ordinary things to happen, when they finally do, it can come as a shock.

Olive's first instinct was to call out for help. But something stopped her. For one thing, she didn't want to cause more trouble for her mother, who already had enough on her plate, what with arranging the funeral and attending to the guests. Grandma Sylvie was the mother of Olive's father, who had followed in her footsteps by becoming an accountant. Olive's parents had divorced when she was very small and her father had spent the last few years working in Australia, visiting his children for a few months every summer. He had been due to come back to England for Grandma Sylvie's funeral, but his flight had been cancelled at the last minute, meaning Olive's mother was left to handle everything alone. And she wasn't happy about it.

This was one reason that Olive didn't call her mother, and the explanation she vowed to give if she were ever questioned. But there was another reason. It was nothing more than a feeling, really. A feeling that the person in the window hadn't waved at Olive just because she happened to be there – but because they had *known* she would be there. That, in fact, they had waited for this precise moment, perhaps when no one else was looking, to get her attention.

If that were the case, it raised several questions in Olive's mind – alongside the obvious one of *what on earth is somebody doing in my grandmother's house?* – such as, *how would anybody know that I watch the house from my bedroom window?* and *why would they try to get my attention in that way?* and *why wouldn't they simply knock on the front door?*

Olive's brain went into overdrive, imagining all the possible answers to these questions. And she knew there was only one way to find out the truth. She leapt off the bed and, closing her bedroom door softly behind her, tiptoed along the hallway. She entered the living room, which she had to go through to get to the front door. Everywhere she looked were groups of chattering cousins and second cousins and aunts and uncles trying not to spill finger food down their funeral outfits. Her brother Frankie was sitting on the sofa, sandwiched between a pair of elderly relatives bickering about politics.

With her long and quick legs, Olive managed to dodge them all as she crossed the room. About halfway to the door, she paused. Displayed on a table in the centre of the living room was a photograph of Grandma Sylvie. It was the kind of photograph you couldn't help but stop to look at.

Unlike Olive, Grandma Sylvie hadn't been particularly tall or broad-shouldered. In fact, she had been quite short and slender. And yet she filled the gold frame with a dominating presence. In the photo, she wore her white hair pinned tightly to her head. Her outfit was just as practical: a boxy, burnt-orange coloured blouse with a bow tied at her neck.

But it was her eyes that really gripped you. They were piercing, following you fiercely around the room in a way that made your posture instantly straighten.

Pressing her shoulders back, Olive nodded respectfully at the portrait, as if to say, *I've got this, Grandma*. Then she slipped out the front door without anybody noticing.

Once outside, there was no sense in waiting around. Olive knew that would only give nerves the chance to set in. So she walked straight over the road, through the creaky garden gate and up the path to the front door, which she found had been left ajar. She hesitated only for a moment as she reached the threshold before pushing the door open and stepping inside her grandmother's house for the very first time.

'Hello?' she called out, as she emerged into a narrow hallway. 'Who's there?' Olive tried her best to sound grown-up and fearless.

When no response came, Olive's resolve faltered. 'I know . . . I know you're here,' she continued. 'I saw you in the window.'

Again, nothing came back. Olive moved slowly down the hallway. As she did, she looked up and down and left and right, taking in everything around her. There was a thick porridge-coloured carpet beneath her feet. The walls were beige, with framed paintings of boats and water-colour fruit bowls hanging along the length of the room.

It was, in other words, an entirely ordinary hallway. A little old-fashioned in the critical eyes of a twelve-year-old, but certainly nothing exceptional. This was a disappointment to Olive, whose imagination about what she might find there had run wild. But then again, she reminded herself, it was only the hallway, and hallways are very rarely exciting places, so Olive continued onwards hopefully.

About halfway along the corridor she came to an open door and stepped through it. Even in the gloomy darkness Olive could see the room on the other side was an explosion of lace and florals. There was peach wallpaper (that is, wallpaper with peaches on) and a flowery green sofa with bright orange cushions. One side of the room was taken up by a huge stone fireplace with a row of nick-nacks on the mantlepiece. A collection of glossy houseplants were situated near the window, which had its lacy curtains drawn, and a thick patterned rug covered yet more carpet. The place had a cosy, lived-in feel, while also being spotlessly tidy.

'Well done, Olive,' came a voice from behind her. 'You came alone. I was rather worried about that.'

Olive whipped her head around. In a dark corner of the room was an armchair, and somebody was sitting in it. This person stared at Olive for a moment, before switching on the lamp beside her.

Olive saw now that the woman was wearing a

maroon velvet suit. Her silver-grey hair was cut sharply to her ears. She was in her late sixties, or so Olive guessed, with eyes that shone behind a pair of purple spectacles. She sat primly in the orange chair, her long slender body contrasting with the lumpy cushions.

'Who . . . who are you?' asked Olive, breaking the silence.

The woman uncrossed her legs and rose to her feet. She shook Olive's hand firmly and motioned that they should sit together on the green flowery sofa. 'My name is Edith Lowry,' she said, brushing down her dress as she seated herself next to Olive. 'You may call me Ms Lowry. I'm a lawyer who had the honour of working for your late grandmother.' Her manner of speaking was abrupt and business-like, as if they were meeting across a boardroom table not a flowery living-room sofa. 'So sorry to wave you over here like that, and on such a sad occasion. It all had to be a little cloak and dagger, for reasons you'll soon understand.'

Olive blinked. It was rather a lot to take in at once. Being inside Grandma Sylvie's house would have been strange enough on its own, without encountering such a person inside. 'It's nice to meet you . . . Ms Lowry,' Olive said, 'but if you don't mind me asking, what are you doing in my grandmother's house? The funeral is being held at my place across the road. Were you given the wrong address?' Her tone was a little more accusatory than politeness should allow. But Olive knew that entering somebody else's house without permission was called trespassing and it was against the law. And as a lawyer, so would Ms Lowry.

'I'm here,' the woman replied crisply, 'at the request of your grandmother.'

Olive's heart began to thump. 'You are?' Her mind raced through possible explanations. 'Why?'

'You need to listen very carefully.' Ms Lowry tapped her fingertips together, as if waiting to confirm whether Olive was indeed listening. When she was satisfied, she continued. 'Your grandmother was a somewhat unusual person. I'm sure I don't have to tell you that. And she was very particular about what she wanted to happen with her belongings after she died. This house, for instance, will go to her son, your father. Most of her money she decided to give to a local cat sanctuary. Those cats will be dining like royalty for some years, let me tell you. But there was something important that your grandmother wanted you, Olive – and you alone – to have. A very special gift.'

Olive shifted her weight. 'A gift?' she repeated, trying not to sound too sceptical. She couldn't imagine for one second what Grandma Sylvie would have wanted to leave her. Leaving all her money to a bunch of cats didn't sound *too* out of character for her grandmother; she'd always doted on her tabby cat, James, who roamed the neighbourhood like an escaped lion. But it made no sense at all for her grandmother to leave Olive a gift. Perhaps there was a mistake, or perhaps Ms Lowry was some kind of scammer? If that was the case, Olive didn't know what she could possibly want to scam from her, but she kept her guard up all the same. 'What kind of gift?' she asked, crossing her legs in a way that she hoped looked grown-up.

Ms Lowry's eyes glinted. 'Something I bet you've never even heard of. Most people haven't, because the technology is new and *very* exclusive. It's made by a company called Forget Me Not, named after the flower, of course.'

With the mention of the words 'new' and 'exclusive' Olive forgot all about keeping her guard up. 'What is it?' she asked, sitting forward.

Ms Lowry smiled, apparently pleased that Olive was finally as interested as she should be. 'It's called a Memoriser. It's a device that allows people to record their memories, and then other people to play them back, and watch them, as if they were their own.

19

Not all their memories, mind. Wouldn't that be boring?' She laughed. 'The person recording them can choose which memories they want to be passed on. In this case, the memories your grandmother wanted *you* to have.'

'*Me*?' replied Olive. 'But why me?'

'I've absolutely no idea.' Ms Lowry shook her head. 'All I know is she was very clear about her wishes. *Olive must get it on the day of my funeral.*'

Olive didn't know which question to ask first. 'How does it work?'

'That part is simple – well, not how it records them – your guess is as good as mine on that – but how you play them back, at least. The Memoriser looks a little like a crown, or a headband. You place it on your head, around your temples, and just above your eyebrows. It has to fit precisely, so all the electronic parts are in contact with your skin. Then you simply close your eyes and clear your mind, as if you were going to sleep. It's best to be lying down somewhere comfortable. Then, when you're completely relaxed, you'll start to see the memories in your mind. It won't be exactly like real life. The smells and sounds will be a little different – a bit duller and less certain. But close enough.'

Olive nodded as if *watching somebody else's memories* was a perfectly normal thing to do. She wished she had a notebook with her, because in her excitement she knew she wouldn't remember everything. Olive could miss entire lessons at school, even if the topic really interested her, because her mind couldn't help wandering. In fact, she'd already stopped listening. Instead, she was imagining herself telling her friends. They probably wouldn't believe her. She bet that *nobody* she knew – nobody in the whole town – had even heard of such a thing.

'There's one other thing,' Ms Lowry continued, interrupting her daydream. 'It *has* to be a secret. It's a condition your grandmother set.'

'Oh,' replied Olive, doing a bad job of hiding her disappointment. 'Of course, I'd never tell a soul . . .'

'Good, because you can only have the memories if you promise that you'll keep all this a secret. Not a word to anyone at school. Not even to your parents.'

Olive swallowed. 'I won't say a word.'

'Very good.' Ms Lowry collected a briefcase beside the armchair and stood. 'Now that's settled, I need to be getting on.'

Olive got up hastily too. 'But wait. Aren't you going to give it to me?' she asked. 'The Memoriser, I mean.'

'No,' Ms Lowry said. She was looking at herself in the mirror over the fireplace. She fixed her hair before taking out a lipstick from a purse inside her briefcase. When she spoke again it was through puckered lips as she covered them with a bright shade of purple. 'It will be delivered to you, securely.'

Olive must have looked worried because Ms Lowry sighed. 'Here, you can take my details.' She produced a card from her purse. 'If you have any burning questions, come visit my office. But please do *try* to use your own initiative first. My time is expensive. The more you waste it, the less smoked salmon those lucky kitties will get to enjoy.'

Olive took the card. A million questions swirled in her head, questions about her grandmother, who she was, what kind of life she'd led. But it seemed their time had run out.

'Take care, Olive,' said Ms Lowry. And with that she snapped her purse shut, turned on her heel and walked out the door.

## CHAPTER THREE

# The Memoriser

Two whole weeks went by without any sign of the Memoriser. Which might as well have been two years for how long it felt to Olive.

Every morning she checked the doormat for post at least three times before going to school. It was the very first thing she did when she got home too. Often, she thought she heard the doorbell ring and ran to answer it, only to find the front porch frustratingly empty. This routine made her jumpy and irritable, which didn't go unnoticed by her family.

'What's got into you?' asked her mother over breakfast one morning after Olive had yet again got up to answer an imaginary doorbell ring. 'You're making me edgy the way you keep jumping up.'

Her brother Frankie was also looking at her with

concern. 'What's with your new obsession with the letterbox?' he said, chomping through a mouthful of cereal. 'Are you expecting something?'

'I'm not obsessed,' replied Olive testily. 'I checked for post a normal amount. Collecting the newspaper and bills and things. It's called being helpful,' she sniffed, unable to look either her mother or brother in the eyes. 'Anyway, are you *sure* that the doorbell is in full working order?'

'Not that again, Olive,' her mother replied. 'There's nothing wrong with the doorbell.'

Olive didn't think it could hurt to have it looked at, but she didn't want to press the point and make her mother even more suspicious. She hadn't forgotten the condition of secrecy that her grandmother had set, though it had been a struggle keeping her promise. Olive wasn't sure how much longer she could last.

As it turned out, the Memoriser didn't arrive in the post like any old parcel would. It was delivered on a Tuesday afternoon as Olive was walking home from school. She had just turned on to the long, busy road that led to the shorter, quieter street where she lived. She was trying to listen to music on her headphones but finding it hard to hear anything above the noisy whoosh of traffic. Admitting defeat, Olive took them off and threw the headphones back into her bag.

It was only then that she realised the rush of traffic wasn't the only noise disturbing her. There was a curious buzzing sound, a humming like a pair of wings beating furiously. Olive looked all around, from left to right, and then, slowly, she looked up. Suspended above her head was either a very small helicopter or a very large insect. It was hovering on the spot, four sets of blades rotating in a blur. Upon being seen, the machine lowered itself until it was floating in the air directly in front of Olive's face.

'OLIVE JONES,' came a soft but nevertheless robotic voice.

'Um . . . yes, hello?' Olive replied. She was, after all, the kind of person who is polite even to inanimate objects.

'VOICE REGONITION COMPLETE. FACIAL SCANNING COMMENCING.'

Before Olive had fully registered what had been said, a beam of white light shone from the machine. It moved in a line up and down her face.

'FACIAL SCANNING COMPLETE,' the voice said. 'IDENTITY OF OLIVE JONES CONFIRMED.'

Olive blinked to clear splotches of light from her eyes. When she could focus again, she saw that the belly of the drone had started to open. A shelf emerged from inside, upon which was a white box.

'PROCEED FOR COLLECTION.' When Olive, who was completely stunned, didn't move, the phrase was repeated. 'PROCEED FOR COLLECTION. PROCEED FOR COLLECTION.'

Snapping out of her trance, Olive grabbed the box. Instantly, the machine closed, lifted into the air, and zoomed off into the sky. Olive watched it climb higher and higher, until it disappeared behind clouds.

As soon as it was out of sight, she turned her attention to the box itself. It wasn't particularly heavy. Someone who didn't know better might have guessed it carried a dozen cupcakes or perhaps a new pair of trainers. There were no markings on the outside, except for a small blue flower on the centre of the lid, which she ran her fingers lightly across. Olive looked around to see if anybody had seen the delivery take place, but the only other pedestrian was a man walking his dog on the opposite side of the road.

'Stop pulling on the lead, Lola!' he was shouting at a racing Bichon Frise. 'Any more of this nonsense and I'll take you straight home!' The dog, a glint of disobedience in her eyes, pulled even harder.

Olive was pretty sure he hadn't noticed anything,

but she decided to race home all the same. Tucking the box under one arm, and trying not to shake it around too much, Olive broke into a jog, not stopping until she got to her front door.

'I'm home,' she called as she opened her front door. 'Anybody there? Mum? Frankie?'

There was no answer. Olive knew her mother wasn't supposed to be home until after work, and that Frankie would be at chess club, but she had wanted to make absolutely sure that the coast was clear. The last thing she needed was difficult questions about where the mysterious white box had come from or what was inside it. Olive shouted once more to be on the safe side. When still no answer came, she shut the front door and hurried to her bedroom.

Once inside her room, Olive set to work. First, she placed the white box carefully on her bedside table. Then she turned on the bedside lamp and drew the curtains. She didn't want any nosy neighbours looking in, after all. When these precautions were complete, Olive sat on her bed and with shaky hands set about opening the box.

The box itself was an ordinary-looking thing, but Olive felt such a jumpy mix of excitement and anxiety when she picked it up that it might have been the world's most valuable diamond, or perhaps a stick of dynamite. To think about what the box actually *contained* – her grandmother's most prized memories – was exceedingly strange. And the fact that Grandma Sylvie had entrusted them to Olive above all others made her aware, suddenly, of a great weight of responsibility.

With a single strip of tape that ran all around the edge removed, she lifted off the lid of the box with surprising ease. Setting it aside, Olive peered at what was held within. Beneath a filling of blue tissue paper, which Olive tore away impatiently, was a hint of something shiny and white. Olive took the strange object out of the box and held it up to the light. It was shaped a bit like a crown or a tiara, just as Ms Lowry had described, and made of a hard, smooth material. If truth be told, Olive was surprised. She'd thought there would be more to it. She had imagined it would be bigger for a start, a complex machine with lots of moving parts and cables all over the place. She'd spent two weeks wondering where she was going to hide it in her bedroom. She needn't have bothered.

Olive turned it over in her hands. It was hard to believe that such a device could do all the things Ms Lowry had said it could. *How does it work?* she wondered. She could see that it was adjustable at the back, so the wearer could fit it to their head. But there were no cables and no 'on' button, either – or, for that matter, any buttons at all. Apart from where you adjusted it, the material was completely smooth all the way round. Rifling through the blue tissue paper for a set of instructions, Olive discovered a single sheet of folded paper at the bottom of the box. But it wasn't instructions. It was a letter, addressed to her. And it was signed by her Grandma Sylvie. Olive was so excited about what the letter might contain that she struggled to read it at first, her brain racing ahead before her eyes could take in the words, which blurred and jumbled on the page. She stopped, took a deep breath, and soon the letters came into focus.

*Dear Olive,*

*If you are reading this letter, you will have received the Memoriser. I had these memories recorded recently, leaving instructions that, in the event of my untimely death, they should be passed to you.*

*You must be a little shocked and confused about why I chose to leave you this device. My reason is simple: I need your help.*

*I will not explain everything within this letter. It would not be safe to do so. Anybody might read it and that would not help our cause. You should also be aware that other people might want to access these memories. This means you must watch them now, without delay. And then you must take action.*

*I can imagine you are still feeling confused. My hope is that once you have seen the memories stored on this device, you will know what you must do. It is a mission that I wish I could have completed a long time ago – a mission which has cast a shadow over my life for some years. Now I must ask you to carry on with my work.*

*Please know that I leave you the Memoriser because I have the utmost confidence in your abilities. I have not had the pleasure of getting to know you like a grandmother should. This is something I regret. But it doesn't mean I haven't taken a keen interest in you, Olive. From afar I have noticed your many fine attributes – your brilliant imagination, your bold instincts – and those of your brother, too – his intelligence and sensitivity. You both make me immensely proud.*

*Knowing what I know about you, here is my advice. Be on your guard always. In this world there are people who wish to claim what isn't theirs. Take help when it's offered, but only from those you trust with your life. If the worst is to happen, do not give up. There are answers out there if you can work out the right place to look – and you have always seemed to know where that place is. A cuddle with James will set you on the right path. Even when defeat seems certain, the game can still be yours to win so long as you plan your next move carefully. Pay little attention to appearances – more often than not, they are deceiving. Never overestimate your enemies. And equally, never underestimate yourself.*

*Good luck.*
*With love and thanks,*
*Grandma Sylvie*


Olive read the letter through three times. She was astonished. In truth, she didn't know which part of the letter she found the most astonishing – that her grandmother was asking for her help with some mysterious task, something she had been unable to achieve in her own lifetime, or that Grandma Sylvie actually *knew* her, was proud of her, even. Knowing this made Olive's cheeks grow red and a warm feeling spread through her. Her grandmother *had* noticed her. She *had* cared. Olive's eyes filled with tears as they lingered over her grandmother's words. With a renewed sense of purpose, and even greater curiosity, she picked up the Memoriser and turned it over in her hands. Grandma Sylvie needed her help. And as she'd instructed, Olive needed to get to work straight away.

*But what do I do with it?* she asked herself, frowning. Olive tried to remember exactly what Ms Lowry had told her two weeks before. She could still hear her voice loud and clear.

*It's best to be lying down somewhere comfortable . . .*

Well, Olive could certainly manage that. At once, she set about arranging and fluffing the pillows on her bed. When she was satisfied, Olive sat back on the mattress. *What else did Ms Lowry say?* she thought, trying to remember.

*You place it on your head, around your temples . . .*

Olive wasn't convinced that simply putting the object on like a hat would make anything happen, but she did as she'd been instructed. The device felt cold against her skin. She fiddled with the back until it fit snugly around her temples.

Olive lay backwards and stared up at the ceiling. She twiddled her thumbs. Nothing happened and she started to feel a bit silly.

*Close your eyes and clear your mind . . .*

She tried to settle her mind, as she'd been told to, pushing away the thoughts that kept racing through her head, like *what are the memories going to look like?* And *what will it feel like to have somebody else's thoughts in my mind?* until eventually the effects of the dim light and the warm bed took hold, and Olive's heartbeat slowed, and her mind started to settle down, along with her breathing. And that's when it started.

Now, memories, like dreams, are difficult things to describe. If you try to put into words what it feels like to *remember* something – your first ever day at school, for instance – you'll see what I mean. You don't watch memories in your head like you'd watch a movie. They don't flutter across your eyelids as if they were projected there. You see them in something called your mind's eye. That's the place inside your head where mental pictures appear. It's the very place, in fact, that you are imagining this story. And *that's* exactly where Olive started to see her grandmother's first memory.

It appeared in her mind's eye gradually, fuzzily. Then the colours got stronger, the shapes became clearer, and the picture grew sharp. It didn't feel exactly like normal life; Olive could tell that what she was seeing wasn't really happening in front of her. But it was awfully close. It was a bit like a very vivid dream – a dream where you've worked out that you're dreaming. A dream where you *could* wake up if you wanted to, but you'd rather it carried on. If you've ever had that experience, then you'll have a good idea what it was like for Olive as the memory drifted into her head.

And so, while she knew that *in real life* she was still lying on her bed, Olive found herself standing in the middle of what looked like a classroom. There were rows of benches and a blackboard at the front. Sitting at the benches were students who looked a little older than she was – about fourteen, she guessed.

Though she was sure she'd never been in that particular room, Olive recognised the set-up well. It was a school science laboratory – or to be more accurate, a memory of one. Olive couldn't help but feel disappointed. If she were to capture her own most prized memories, school science lessons definitely wouldn't be high on the list. In fact, they were moments she'd most like to forget, given the trouble she tended to get herself into, usually by spilling dangerous chemicals or causing mild explosions. *Why did Grandma Sylvie want to capture a memory like this?* she wondered. But before she could ponder this any further, Olive froze at the sound of a voice coming from the front of the classroom.

'Miss Jones!' roared the man sitting in front of the blackboard. His gruff voice had a strange echoey quality. 'What in heavens were you thinking?' He was looking directly at Olive.

For a split second, Olive forgot that she was in a memory. It felt just like when teachers shouted at *her* at school. A familiar jolt of fear travelled through her body. She was already thinking up excuses, when it occurred to Olive that she couldn't possibly be the Miss Jones in trouble – not this time. It was her grandmother who was in the firing line.

'You. Let. The. Frogs. Go.' The teacher at the front of the class, a tall man with a long auburn beard, practically spat the words out. 'You released them – all of them – into the playground.'

The whole class was staring right at Olive now – or

rather they were staring at Grandma Sylvie. Olive realised with a start that she was seeing the scene through Grandma Sylvie's eyes – in fact, she was in Grandma Sylvie's body! The teacher continued, working himself up into an even greater rage. 'You broke into this laboratory at lunchtime, entering a room full of dangerous equipment and volatile substances without permission, and stole school property!'

Olive held her breath. No reply came – and nobody in the class moved. The teacher gave an exasperated groan. 'Can you at least tell me, Sylvie, *why* you decided to take up this little mission of yours?'

This time there was a reply, but not from Sylvie. One of the students in the front row answered. 'She told me it was because you were planning to dissect them, sir.'

A murmur of discussion rippled through the classroom. This was clearly too much for the teacher to take. 'Out!' he yelled. 'Sylvie Jones, get out of my laboratory!'

At exactly this moment, the memory began to wisp away, dissolving into darkness like an evening fog that suddenly clears. And then, as quickly as it had appeared, the memory was gone. Barely a second passed before another memory began to appear in

Olive's mind's eye. This time, Olive found herself in a small office. Olive knew this set-up well too. It was exactly like the times she herself had been sent to the headteacher's office. In fact, Olive instantly felt a wave of guilt come over her. Looking down at herself, Olive realised her grandmother's legs were much longer than they'd been in the previous memory. She must have jumped forwards in time. *But still getting herself into trouble – just like me!* thought Olive. *Is this what Grandma Sylvie wanted me to know? That we're alike?*

Sitting across a desk from Olive was a man wearing a chequered suit. He had a greyish bouffant hairstyle and a crumpled expression on his face.

'We don't enjoy expelling students, Sylvie,' he began in a disappointed tone, 'but we see little point in trying to educate students who don't wish to be educated. What do you have to say about that?' There was silence. 'Nothing at all,' he said, tutting. 'And there we have the problem. Very well!' The man sighed deeply. 'You're only sixteen. You have a long life ahead of you and I wish you the best of luck with it. Although I fear with a start like this you won't make very much of yourself, Sylvie Jones.'

He held out a hand to be shaken. Olive waited

eagerly for what came next. Would her grandmother shake his hand? Would she beg to keep her place at school? But Olive never found out. Instead, there was a noise – an almighty crash. Olive knew instinctively that the noise wasn't a part of the memory. She knew it in the same way that you know your alarm clock going off isn't part of your dream – it simply didn't belong there. A jumble of colours started flashing before her eyes. Memories were beginning and then ending at great speed. It felt like watching a film that was skipping through scenes, getting faster and faster. At the same time, Olive was distantly aware of noises – sounds she was certain didn't belong to the memories.

And then, without warning, everything stopped. All Olive could see now was darkness. Nothing happened for several moments. It took a few seconds more for Olive to come back to herself, and when she did, it felt as if she was waking from a very vivid dream. Slowly she opened her eyes and saw her bedroom ceiling above her. Olive's head scrambled to make sense of what had happened. She was still lying on her bed; she knew that much. She'd been watching her grandmother's memories – but something had gone wrong. The Memoriser had started to malfunction. Then it had stopped completely.

Olive put her hands to her head to feel for the Memoriser. With a surge of terror, followed by a sickening feeling in her belly, she realised it was gone. Olive sat bolt upright. She patted desperately at her head as if, somehow, she'd missed it. Then she searched her bed and the floor beneath it, in case the machine had slipped off as she'd come back around. But it was nowhere to be seen. It didn't make sense. How could the Memoriser have disappeared?

That moment there was another loud crash. This one shook away the remains of Olive's sleepy confusion. Suddenly she was alert and clear-headed. Olive leapt off the bed. There was no mistaking it: *there was someone inside her house.*

Olive ran to her bedroom door, which she noticed was slightly open, though she knew without a doubt that she'd closed it. Quickly, she hurried down the hallway, across the living room, and towards the front door, which like her bedroom door was now open. It didn't occur to Olive that she should be cautious, that there might be danger waiting for her. She'd have time to think about that later – in this moment Olive was guided only by instinct. She raced out of the front door just in time to glimpse a figure dashing round the corner at the end of the street. They were so fast that a glimpse was all she got, not enough to see their face or get a good look at their clothing.

The realisation hit her suddenly. A thief had broken into her house. They had come into her room. *They had stolen the Memoriser!* Her gift from her grandmother. And now, they were getting away with it.

Olive charged down the street after the intruder. She had never run so fast in all her life. Her legs, her lungs burned with the effort. But as fast as she was, by the time she reached the end of the street and turned the corner, the figure was nowhere to be seen.

It took a few seconds, standing in the empty street, for what had happened to sink in. It couldn't be . . . it couldn't. But it was.

The Memoriser was gone.

# CHAPTER FOUR

## James's Secret

When things go very wrong, as they sometimes do, it can be tempting to hope that somebody else will swoop in as if from nowhere and fix everything. There comes a time in everyone's life, however, when the realisation sinks in that *you* must be the one who does the fixing.

Standing on the doorstep of her house, having watched a thief disappear with her grandmother's memories, Olive had exactly this realisation. The anguish of the loss settled in her stomach like a brick. There was nobody who was going to fix this – nobody else who was going to save the day. Calling her mother for help wasn't an option. To tell her about the thief, Olive would have to also tell her about the Memoriser, which she had sworn not to. *Olive* had to do something. *She* had to get the memories back.

Making a plan of action is always important in these kinds of situations. And often the best plans are those which develop in the spur of the moment. Olive could have spent hours plotting and mulling over what to do next, had she been that kind of person. But she wasn't. Instead, she followed her instincts.

Rushing back inside her house, Olive made straight for her grandmother's letter, which had been swept on to the floor in the commotion. She snatched it up and began combing through her grandmother's words. She was sure she remembered a part about things going wrong. Olive traced her finger over the letter line by line until she got to it. *If things go wrong, don't give up. There are answers out there if you can work out the right place to look.* Olive read this line with a sigh of frustration. It didn't seem to help her at all. In fact, if Olive knew where the right place to look for answers was, she wouldn't need to *look* for them in the first place. It was a bit like when you've lost something and some bright spark asks you: *where did you last see it?* It nearly always makes you want to shout something rude back at them.

Olive read the next line of the letter. *A cuddle with James will set you on the right path.* This line had struck her as odd the first time she'd read it. You didn't have to know Grandma Sylvie well to know that it was out of character for her. She hadn't been the cuddly kind of grandmother – and James wasn't the cuddly kind of cat. Olive was sure if she tried to give him a hug she'd end up with a set of deep scratches. That wasn't to say Grandma Sylvie wasn't very fond of the cat. After long weeks away, she'd always greet the stocky tabby warmly on her return. A few times Olive had seen the cat accept a scratch under the chin, but nothing more affectionate than that.

So why would her grandmother have encouraged her to try to cuddle a cat like James? It made no sense whatsoever. She read the letter again to make absolutely sure she'd understood correctly. *A cuddle with James will set you on the right path*. This time it made her laugh out loud. There was no doubt about it, there was something very strange about such a suggestion. A thought suddenly occurred to Olive. What if *that* was the point? What if Grandma Sylvie had intended to write something that would stand out to Olive as completely ridiculous. Perhaps . . . it was a clue!

With a flash of concern, Olive realised that she hadn't seen James for some weeks now, not since before Grandma Sylvie's funeral. Usually, the cat spent his time lurking in the bungalow's front garden pouncing on unsuspecting dandelions. Olive leaned on her bed and peered through the window. After a few moments of frantic searching, her heart in her throat, at last she spotted it – there, just visible above the long grass of her grandmother's overgrown front garden, she could see a quick flame-like swish of tail.

Olive breathed a sigh of relief.

Following her hunch, she folded the letter and put it in her trouser pocket. Then she set off, first to the kitchen, and then out the front door and across the road towards the bungalow opposite.

'James!' she called as she approached the creaky gate and entered the front garden. 'Come here, boy.'

A rustling in the grass let Olive know she'd been heard. Moments later, the cat emerged on the path that led to the front door. He eyed Olive with a look of deep suspicion.

'Hi there, James. What have you been up to, all alone?'

The cat responded with stony silence. Olive made kissing noises to encourage him closer. James weaved through the grass, approaching warily, as if deciding whether or not to pounce.

'Look, what's this?' she said in a singsong voice. 'I have some chicken for you. Come on, how about it?' Olive dangled a slice of chicken in the air. James froze. Olive flung the treat on to the path in front of her, and the cat pounced. When he looked up, licking his lips, it was as if the chicken had evaporated.

'Good boy, James. That's it. Want a little more?' The cat looked back at her with green, insistent eyes. 'Come a bit closer then . . . that's it.'

The cat did as she asked, and Olive tossed another chicken slice his way. She smiled, delighted that her plan was working. This time, when the cat looked up for more, she noticed something she hadn't before. He was wearing a collar. Now, this might have been an ordinary thing for another cat. But it certainly wasn't for James. He was not the kind of cat who would tolerate the indignity of wearing a collar. This was a cat who considered himself more of a lion than a tabby. And lions do *not* wear collars.

With another piece of chicken – the last she had – Olive coaxed the cat even closer. Then, having shown him her now empty hands, she carefully gave his chin a gentle stroke, exactly like her grandmother used to do. To her relief, the cat didn't dart away, but began to purr appreciatively. As soon as she felt she could

45

get away with it, Olive gently rotated his collar until she came to where the name tag should be. And as she did so, Olive gave a small gasp. In place of a name tag was a set of two keys, attached by a clip.

James gave a low meow, as if congratulating Olive for finally making the discovery. As gently as she could, Olive unclipped the collar from around the cat's thick neck. He shook himself gratefully. Then he was off, shooting through the long grass and disappearing under the neighbour's neatly shaped hydrangea.

Standing in front of her grandmother's house, Olive inspected the keys carefully. One was bronze and about the length of her finger. The other was silver and shaped like a lightning bolt with a button at the top. Olive couldn't believe it, but her suspicions had been right. Her grandmother *had* left her a clue. She'd mentioned James in the letter so that Olive would discover the keys. Now all Olive had to do was to work out what the keys were for. And she had a strong hunch that she wouldn't need to go far.

She thought back to another line in the letter. *There are answers out there if you can work out the right place to look – and you have always seemed to know where that place is.* At first this line had frustrated Olive; it had seemed like her grandmother was pointing out the obvious. But perhaps, like the line about James, it had a hidden meaning. Perhaps it was another clue. Olive thought about how often she'd watched her grandmother's bungalow from her bedroom window. She'd always believed it was her secret, that nobody else in the world had known. But had Grandma Sylvie known all that time? *You have always seemed to know where that place is.* Checking the letter again, Olive felt certain now. She knew exactly what she had to do.

Olive set her sights on the bungalow's front door. She could tell without even trying that the silver key wasn't the one she needed. It was the wrong shape and type for a door – it seemed more like a fancy car key. With a deep breath, she tried the bronze key instead. It fitted in the lock perfectly.

Grinning, Olive turned the key and pushed the door open. She had one foot already inside the house when a voice from behind made her freeze.

'Olive?'

Inside she gave a groan. It was a voice she knew well – very well. And it belonged to her brother. What was he doing there? He was meant to be at chess club for at least another hour. Slowly, Olive turned on the spot.

'Hi, Frankie.' She tried to sound like she had nothing to hide. 'You're home early.'

'Chess club was cancelled this week . . .' he said distractedly. He was starting at her with a look of astonishment. 'What . . . what are you doing?' he asked. 'How did you get a key to Grandma Sylvie's bungalow?'

Olive searched her brain for believable excuses and could find none. She briefly considered telling him a version of the truth – that she had got the key from James and leaving out everything that came before. Then she reconsidered. It would sound ridiculous. Her brother would think she was making up stories. It would have to be all or nothing. A part of Olive wanted to tell her brother to mind his own business and send him straight home. Another part was longing to spill the beans and tell him everything that had happened over the last couple of weeks.

As Olive deliberated between these two options, she thought back to what her grandmother had written in the letter. *Take help when it's offered, but only from those you trust with your life.* Her brother wasn't exactly offering help. But that wasn't to say she didn't need it. After all, she had a lot to deal with all on her own. Taking possession of the Memoriser had been a huge weight on her shoulders. Now that it

48

had been stolen, that weight felt like it had doubled.

At the same time, Olive wasn't sure that her brother would even want to help her. They weren't as close these days as they had once been. Besides, Frankie *hated* getting into trouble. There was a chance he'd run straight home to call their mother and spoil the whole thing. Olive looked at him carefully. His small, inquisitive face peered up at her, blinking with confusion. Though they had their differences, Frankie was the most trustworthy person she knew. He hardly ever lied and never about important things. Olive knew she could trust him completely. She could *trust him with her life.*

Taking a deep breath, she pulled their grandmother's front door closed again. 'Listen, Frankie. There's something I need to tell you.' She stared at him seriously. 'But first you're going to want to sit down.'

She sank down on to the porch step and patted the place next to her, and her brother, looking more puzzled than ever before, came and sat beside her uncertainly. And then, there on their grandmother's front step, Olive told Frankie everything.

Frankie's eyes got wider and wider as the story went on. When she came to the end of the tale, Olive reached into her pocket and pulled out the letter.

'Grandma wrote a letter explaining everything. Or almost everything, anyway. From what she's written, I think that she expected me to tell you about the Memoriser at some point. That she even wanted me to. So that we could help her with her mission – whatever it is – together.'

Frankie let out his breath with a low whistle. Olive eyed him nervously. She knew from her own experience that this would be a lot for him to take in. After a few seconds, he took the letter from her hands and scanned the words. He opened his mouth as if to say something, then closed it again.

After a thoughtful pause, he finally spoke. 'So, Grandma Sylvie left you her memories. Then as soon as they arrived, somebody stole them.' His wide eyes were fixed steadily on the stone path ahead. 'That still doesn't explain how you got the key,' he said, looking across at her.

Olive had to laugh. Her brother was always so practical. 'You won't believe me, but it was on James's collar.'

Frankie laughed too and shook his head. 'I suppose it's not the most unbelievable thing out of everything you've just told me. So were you planning to just let yourself in?'

Olive pointed to the letter. 'If I'm going to work out what this mission is, Grandma Sylvie's house is the first place I need to look. It's why she left the keys with James, I think.'

To Olive's surprise, Frankie rose to his feet. 'We'd better get started then. It will be easier if we look together.'

'You'll help?'

'It's like you said – Grandma wanted us to work together.' He shrugged. 'So let's get going.'

Olive grinned at her brother as together they stood and let themselves into their grandmother's house. It felt like an invisible weight had been lifted off her shoulders as they walked into the beige corridor together. Keeping her unusual inheritance a secret for the last two weeks had been difficult. It felt so much better to now be sharing the burden.

Once inside, the siblings got to work immediately, heading straight down the hallway and into the living room, which seemed as good a place as any to start. What exactly she was expecting to find in Grandma Sylvie's home, Olive couldn't say. She was hoping for more clues – a diary, or another letter perhaps – which might help to unlock the secrets of her grandmother's mysterious life and reveal who might have wanted to steal her memories. She didn't know where such things might be hidden and so they looked everywhere. Olive picked up china trinkets and figurines on the mantlepiece. Frankie inspected vases and potted plants. Together they rifled through papers in the mahogany bureau and pulled books out of the bookcase. Olive even checked under the rug and underneath the wooden coffee table. When one of them thought of a new place to search, Olive felt a surge of excitement. *This could be it*, she thought, but each time they found nothing but dust or the occasional lost penny.

When they'd searched the kitchen, the bedroom and the bathroom and still not found anything, Olive began to panic. Perhaps her plan hadn't been such a good one after all. Perhaps she shouldn't have rushed to act and should instead have taken the time to think things through. Her teachers were always telling her to think before she acted. Now a knot of guilt was beginning to form in her stomach. What if her grandmother *hadn't* wanted her to search the bungalow after all? What if Olive was only finding an excuse to snoop around – getting carried away with her imagination like she always did? It was, after all, a terrible invasion of Grandma Sylvie's privacy to go through her things like this.

Stomping back into the living room with a loud sigh, Olive slumped down on to the slouchy orange armchair, the one she'd found Ms Lowry sitting in two weeks earlier. 'We're not getting anywhere, Frankie. I must have been wrong . . . wrong about everything.'

'Come on, don't give up yet.' He was pushing his head into the fireplace and craning his neck to look up the chimney. 'We have to be missing something,' he said, his voice echoing as he spoke.

Olive pulled a lacy cushion to her chest and hugged it tightly. All she'd wanted since she'd found out about the Memoriser was to get to know her grandmother. So far, she had failed miserably.

And yet, settled in the warmth of her grandmother's armchair, Olive felt closer to her than she ever had before. It must have been somewhere she had sat often, Olive thought, judging by the wear in the fabric. It smelled like she used to smell, too – of an old-fashioned, floral perfume. Olive imagined her sitting in this very spot over the years and wondered if she'd ever felt lonely. This was a new thought for Olive. Up till now, she'd only really thought about what *she'd* missed out on as a result of not having a regular grandmother. She hadn't given much thought to how it might have made Grandma Sylvie feel, to be so near to her family and yet so distant from them too.

*What should I do, Grandma?* she thought desperately. *How can I get your memories back?*

At that moment, Olive became aware of something jabbing into her side. She reached down and dislodged the culprit – a small remote control, attached to the chair by a cord. The chair was a recliner, the kind that flips backwards and unfolds like a bed. She'd seen them before advertised on television. Olive cast her eyes distractedly over the remote. The remote control wasn't at all what she'd expected it to be. It only had the one button – a huge gold one with the letters *S.J.* printed in black across the centre. Olive recognised these letters instantly as her grandmother's initials. But why, she wondered, would a remote control for a chair have her grandmother's initials on it?

Olive swept her finger across the button gently. 'Hey, Frankie. Come here a sec and take a look at this.'

'What is it?' came his muffled voice from inside the fireplace.

Now most people – even adults – when they see an inviting-looking button, find it hard to resist pressing it, and Olive didn't have particularly strong impulse control at the best of times. She could practically hear the button crying out for her to push it. And so that's exactly what she did.

A strange noise began beneath her. It was the sound of gears grinding, mechanics whirring.

'What's that noise?' said Frankie, getting his head out of the fireplace at last.

'It's Grandma's armchair,' Olive shouted back, as the noise got louder. 'It has a button with—'

But that was all she had time to say. For the very next moment, the faded orange armchair dropped through the floor, with Olive along for the ride.

## CHAPTER FIVE

# The Basement

The armchair plummeted as if the ground beneath it had suddenly vanished. It wasn't free-falling as such. It was more like a lift that had been set to hyper-speed.

Olive scrunched her eyes tightly shut, clinging to the arms of the chair in terror. If Olive had opened her eyes, she would have seen a square of light above her getting smaller as she descended further into darkness. It was hard to know exactly how far she was falling; she only knew that she couldn't let go. After what seemed like for ever, but was probably a matter of seconds, the armchair started to slow before coming to a less than gentle stop.

Olive opened her eyes slowly. It felt like her stomach had been flipped like a pancake. She still had the sensation of falling, despite now being on firm ground. As soon as the feeling passed, she leaped out of the armchair as quickly as if it was on fire. For all Olive knew, the chair could drop again at any moment and she wasn't going to stick around for a second ride.

'Frankie?' she spluttered, calling up to the small square of light now far above her.

Just then, a line of lights built into the walls flashed on. Now Olive could see where she'd landed. She gasped. It was nothing like the living room she'd just been sitting in, with its dated patterns and lacy curtains. She was standing in a long, spacious open-plan room. It had the feel of a very stylish office, with gunmetal-grey walls and a concrete floor. There were no windows – Olive could tell she was underground – but it was far from dingy. Everything was beautiful, modern, sleek. It reminded her of the kind of place that existed in movies but never in real life.

She glanced back at the worn-out armchair she'd just vacated. Upstairs, in the flowery living room, the chair had fitted in completely. Now, against its new backdrop, it looked ridiculous. Without warning the armchair started moving shakily upwards. Before Olive could do a thing about it, the chair was high above her head, ascending towards the living room. It vanished through the hole in the ceiling and then a moment later, both the hole and the chair were gone.

'Frankie!' Olive shouted, not knowing whether her brother could hear her.

For several seconds, nothing happened. Olive stared upwards, biting her lip as panic built inside her. Was she trapped here now? How would she get out? Then, to her relief, she heard a noise like a hatch opening. The square of light appeared again as the bottom of the armchair began descending towards her. Olive saw white trainers dangling over the seat cushion as the chair slowly approached the ground. She jumped out of the way. As Frankie landed, his eyes were impossibly wide. He got to his feet and rushed towards his sister, clutching her around the middle. 'You disappeared through the floor!'

'I know!' She laughed, hugging him back. Both were shaking slightly with the rush of it all. 'But just look at this place!'

Olive tried to calm herself down as she walked over to a curved black desk with a high-backed leather chair tucked under it, her footsteps loud on the hard floor.

On the wall behind the desk were several huge

computer screens, which had all come to life with the lights. Some had complex graphs with luminous zigzagging lines. Others had nothing but letters and strange symbols. On one of the screens, she saw a map of the world. On another there was what looked like a blueprint of a building. Olive tried to make sense of the jumble, but quickly gave up. Together the glow of the screens gave the room an eerie blue tinge.

'I didn't think Grandma Sylvie even knew how to use a computer,' Olive said with astonishment.

'Yeah . . . or how to play chess.' Frankie pointed towards a small sitting area beside the desk where a chessboard was laid out between two chairs. 'It looks like the game has been abandoned just before the end. White is about to win by a landslide.'

'I wonder who she was playing with,' said Olive. This was an odd question for both of them to consider. Neither had ever noticed their grandmother having visitors round – but, then again, there was clearly a lot they didn't know about her. They'd never have guessed, for instance, that she spoke more than one language. And yet nearby was a bookcase filled with thick tomes written in more languages than either of them could name.

'Look! There's even a gym,' said Frankie. Sure

enough, across the room was a collection of weights, the bulky kind that you might see heaved around in the Olympics. There was a well-beaten punchbag too, and other equipment like skipping ropes and a rowing machine.

Olive shook her head with disbelief. 'I knew Grandma liked to keep fit but this . . .'

As she made her way towards the weights for a closer look, she knocked against something hanging from the ceiling. Looking up, Olive saw a series of targets screwed into the concrete above, each one hanging at a different height and heavily punctured at the bullseye. The children gazed at them with disbelief.

A secret basement . . . multiple computers . . . gym equipment . . . and now targets. The evidence was building in Olive's head about who her grandmother had really been. She wondered whether Frankie was thinking the same but, like her, was too embarrassed to say it out loud.

There was a line of bulky metal lockers near the hanging targets. Most were shut and heavily padlocked, but there was one that was slightly ajar, and Olive gently nudged it farther open, wondering if maybe her grandma had left it open on purpose for them. Inside was a set of walkie-talkies, some wigs in varying colours, a pair of fake moustaches and stick-on eyebrows (the kind that could be used to disguise a person's appearance), a special kite (which according to its packaging could be used to survey surroundings from above), and a small football that the label advised was mildly explosive when kicked. Frankie prised open the locker next to it and found what looked like a plastic pistol, which on closer inspection they saw contained darts with GPS trackers.

'Cool,' Frankie whispered under his breath. 'But . . . what was Grandma Sylvie *doing* with all this stuff?'

'I don't know,' Olive replied, 'but I have a feeling she wasn't an accountant.'

As they walked past the line of lockers, they noticed that on the back wall tucked behind the lockers was a doorway.

Olive tried the door – it was open. They stepped cautiously through it into the next room, and as they did, lights above their head automatically came to life. Frankie audibly gasped. This room was smaller than the last, and sitting at the centre, gleaming under yellowish lighting, was a car.

It wasn't just any old car, either. It was an impossibly shiny one, with a sleek metallic blue body and a sparkling silver grille. Olive could instantly tell that it was one of the driverless cars she'd been hearing about recently. Their mum had been watching a documentary about them on the television the other night. She'd never actually seen one for herself. And it was a thing of beauty. Opposite the car was what looked like a garage door. Being underground, Olive was confused by this. Where could such a door possibly lead to? How could the car ever get up to street level? But then again, had she not been standing inside it, Olive would have thought the existence of the basement itself was impossible.

Glancing over at Frankie, she saw the dazed look on his face. 'I don't believe it . . .' he spluttered, reaching out to touch the car's glossy body. 'I didn't know Grandma Sylvie could drive. What was she doing with a car like *this*? I mean . . . the gym . . . the computers . . . this *car*! It's like Grandma Sylvie was some kind of . . .'

He trailed off and the pair stood in silence.

'. . . it's like she was some kind of spy, Frankie,' Olive finished. 'That's what we're both thinking, isn't it?'

Frankie was silent. He ran his hands over the car's glossy body, checking the doors and finding them all locked, to his disappointment.

Olive reached into her pocket and pulled out her grandmother's letter. 'It all makes sense,' she said. 'I mean, who has "missions" apart from spies? We just need to figure out what the mission *was*. If I still had her memories, it would be easy . . .' she went on, pacing up and down the concrete floor in frustration, 'but I think Grandma must have guessed someone would be after the memories, so she left us other clues in the letter just in case. Like what she said about cuddling James. I *knew* that had to mean something because *no way* she'd recommend it otherwise. And she told me to ask for help but only from someone I trust with my life . . .'

Frankie looked at her with a grin. 'And that made you confide in me, which was *definitely* good advice. So, I think you're probably on to something.'

'Maybe there are more clues in here,' said Olive, reading over the last lines of the letter again. 'Listen here. Grandma wrote, '*Even when defeat seems certain, the game can still be yours to win. So long as you plan your next move carefully.*'

Frankie frowned. 'What does *that* mean?'

'I've got no idea,' admitted Olive. 'I mean, this isn't exactly a game like Monopoly, is it?'

Suddenly, Frankie's eyes lit up. 'Hang on!'

Without another word, he headed back into the other room. Olive followed after him. He was standing over the chess board.

'Remember what I said when I first saw this?' Frankie asked her.

'Yeah, you said it looked like this game was pretty much over . . .' Olive trailed off. '*Even when defeat seems certain*!' Olive said, reciting the line from the letter as she realised what Frankie was hinting at.

'Exactly!' Frankie said triumphantly. 'There are loads more white pieces on the board than black pieces – it looks like white is about to win, but . . . how does that bit of the letter end again?'

'. . . *the game can still be yours to win. So long as you plan your next move carefully*,' Olive recited dutifully. She examined the board but it told her nothing. She'd never much liked chess after once getting into trouble at school for hiding pieces in her socks.

Instead, she watched Frankie. There was a look of deep concentration on his face as he stared at the board, muttering under his breath in the way he did when trying to untangle a riddle in his head. 'I see it!' he said finally. 'If the black knight moves over there, then it's check mate. The game is over. And against the odds, black will have won. All with one move.'

Looking deeply satisfied, Frankie picked up the knight and made the game-winning move, putting the knight down on to its new square.

There was a loud *click*. Then, without warning, from the side of the chess board, something sprang outwards. Frankie jumped backwards.

Olive gasped. 'A secret compartment!'

Pride mingled with the surprise on Frankie's face as he caught on to what had happened. 'I did it . . . I solved one of Grandma's clues! All by myself!'

Olive smiled and clapped him on the back. 'Lucky you're here! I would *never* have got that.'

Frankie beamed. 'Do you think . . . that was a clue especially for me? That Grandma put it into the letter because she knew you'd ask me for help and only I'd be able to figure it out?'

Olive ruffled his dark hair fondly. 'I'm certain that she did,' she said softly. 'I'm starting to think she knew us both better than either of us realised.' There was a brief silence between them. 'Now come on,' she went on, 'let's see what's inside.'

Olive carefully pulled the hidden compartment fully open to examine its contents. Stashed inside the wooden drawer was a stack of grey folders. Resting on top of the pile was another single sheet of folded paper. This time, Olive recognised the swirl of her grandmother's handwriting at once. Sitting beside this was an antique-looking gold watch, one that Olive had seen their grandmother often wear.

'Look!' she exclaimed. 'Another letter from Grandma!'

Frankie craned his neck over his sister's shoulder. 'Read it out loud. It could contain more clues!'

*Dear Olive and Frankie,*

*You have come this far – well done. I was sure that together you would decipher the clues I left behind in my last letter. By now I'm also sure you will have realised something else. That for as long as you have known me, and for many years before, I have lived a life of secrets. The life – no doubt you will have already guessed – of a spy.*

*I wish I could have told you both about this before now. I trust that you understand why I could not. And that I wouldn't be telling you now if it wasn't vitally important that I do so. The reason – as you already know – is that I need your help.*

*For many years now, it has felt like a*

*shadow has been following my every move. Secrets from my most covert intelligence operations have found their way to people who should never have known them. This has put my career, and many lives, at risk – including my own. Given the nature of the secrets they have stolen, I am sure that the person responsible – who I have given the code name SHADOW – is somebody close to me. Somebody who is working, or used to work, or is close to someone who works for the British Intelligence Service. This would make the culprit what we in the intelligence industry call 'a mole'. I'm also certain that, for Shadow to target me like they have, their motive must have been personal, at least at first, though I also suspect that now it has become about something else, something bigger than me.*

*Over the last thirteen years, I've been working secretly to uncover the identity of Shadow. On several occasions I've come close to doing so, and yet never close enough. Now, I'm afraid that I'm running out of time. I can no longer be sure that I'll be able to complete my mission. Asking for help from colleagues at the* agency is not an option. How can I know who to trust? This means that I have no choice but to leave the mission with the only two people in the world who I trust without question.

This is you – my grandchildren. When I am gone, I must ask you to use my memories – which may hold a clue that I've missed – and the information contained within these files to finish what I started. You will not be starting from scratch. I have narrowed down the identity of Shadow to four suspects. Within these files you will find everything you need to know about them. Study the dossiers carefully, make a plan, and then get straight to work. Leave no stone unturned. The devious actions of Shadow are a threat to national security. If they remain undetected, the country will never truly be safe – you, my grandchildren, will never truly be safe.

Take care of each other, and good luck

Grandma Sylvie

P.S. Olive, I hope you'll look after my favourite wristwatch for me. It runs a little slow, but it still has its uses.

Olive and Frankie looked at each other, their eyes wide.

Frankie was the first to speak, staring at the letter as if it were on fire. 'We were right about the spy thing, then.'

Olive looked down at the four grey folders. Stamped across the top of each one in black ink were the words **MISSION SHADOW**.

Frankie, meanwhile, had begun to pace backwards and forwards anxiously. 'I don't know how I feel about all this, Olive. This mission . . . it sounds dangerous.'

'Let's just look at the files and think things through, like Grandma said we should.' Olive picked up her grandmother's chunky gold watch and clasped the cold metal around her wrist, enjoying the satisfying weight of it. 'We can make a plan and then—'

'A *plan*?' Frankie cut in. 'We can't make a *plan*. We shouldn't be getting involved with any of this! It's too risky. Grandma Sylvie should never have even asked.'

'You heard what Grandma wrote. She had no choice. Besides. She *believed* in us. She *trusted* us.'

Frankie sighed. 'She hardly knew us,' he said quietly, looking down at the floor.

Olive was starting to feel a familiar prickle at the

back of her neck. Whenever she lost her temper that was always how it started. 'Grandma knew enough about us to know that *you'd* work out her chess clue. And that *I* used to watch her bungalow from my bedroom window. *And* that we'd work best as a team.' She put a hand on her brother's arm, but he didn't respond. 'Although maybe she was wrong about that last one,' Olive finished angrily.

Frankie looked up at her. A hurt expression washed over his face and Olive instantly regretted what she'd said.

'Even if we wanted to, we can't complete Mission Shadow now anyway,' Frankie shot at her, before she could offer an apology. 'The clues were in her memories. And in case you've forgotten, the Memoriser was stolen.'

A frustrated noise came from Olive's throat. 'And who do you think *stole* the Memoriser?'

Frankie's eyes widened. 'You think . . . you think . . . the mole? The person Grandma called Shadow?'

'Precisely!' said Olive triumphantly. 'That Memoriser would have been *full* of clues about their identity. They couldn't have risked someone seeing them.'

Frankie went quiet. Olive carried on.

'And if the mole – Shadow – thinks we've seen her

memories, we're *already* in danger. They know where we live. There's nothing to stop them coming back.'

Frankie shivered. 'But what can we do now? The memories are gone!'

'We haven't lost *all* the clues, remember? We might not have her memories, but we still have these dossiers that Grandma left us.' She pointed to the drawer. 'And we have each other. I know that we can work it out if we work together. We'll complete the mission. We'll stop Shadow once and for all. *And* we'll get Grandma's memories back. Come on, we have to! For Grandma Sylvie.'

Frankie sighed. After a moment, he said, 'You're going to do this with or without me, aren't you?'

'Yes,' said Olive firmly.

Frankie nodded. 'OK, I'm in. For Grandma Sylvie.'

# CHAPTER SIX

# Mission Shadow

Leaning palms-down on her grandmother's desk, Olive surveyed the four grey folders, which she'd splayed out in front of them.

Taking a deep breath, she got ready to open the first folder. She had always been exceptionally good at working out the mysteries in films or television. She could often figure out who the guilty suspect was before the detective did. And she always spotted a plot twist coming from a mile off. It was a skill she took great pride in and one that mostly annoyed her family, because she tended to spoil the endings of things. Until now though, her skills had never been put to the test on a real-life mystery.

'So,' she began, trying her best to hide her self-doubt from her brother, 'if I've learned anything from films, it's that there are three things we need to be watching out for.'

'OK, what are they?' asked Frankie, looking worried.

'Motive, means and opportunity,' she replied, counting them out on her fingers. 'Take *motive*, to start with. We need to work out whether any of these suspects had a reason to steal secrets from Grandma Sylvie. It could have been just about making money, but there was probably more to it. Jealousy, greed . . . or something else. Grandma did say after all that she thought it must be personal.' Olive had started walking backwards and forwards in front of her brother, the way a teacher might pace when trying to impart a particularly important lesson. Truth be told, she was rather enjoying herself now. 'Then we need to work out whether any of the suspects had the *means* to be Shadow. That's just about working out whether they had the right tools or skills to do the job. I bet they would need to have exceptional spy skills, for instance.'

Olive looked over at her brother to make sure he was following, and he gave her a nod, so she went on.

'Lastly, there's *opportunity*, which is about whether they even had the chance to steal secrets from

Grandma Sylvie. They couldn't have stolen the Memoriser if they didn't know about it, for instance, or if they have a strong alibi for this afternoon.'

'Motive . . . means . . . and opportunity. Got it!' said Frankie, who looked like he was wishing he had a pen and paper to take notes.

'OK, now let's see what we can find out about the four suspects.' Olive pointed at the folder nearest Frankie. 'Starting with that one.'

Frankie picked up the folder and carefully peeled back its front cover. His face took on a look of surprise at what he saw inside. 'It's an old lady with silver hair,' he said, 'who must *really* like the colour purple.'

'What?' Olive said urgently, making Frankie flinch. 'Did you say purple?'

Olive whipped the folder out of Frankie's hands before he could protest. She found herself staring at a photograph of a woman with short silver hair, purple lipstick and a lilac jacket. Olive recognised her at once.

EDITH LOWRY

'You didn't have to snatch it,' Frankie said sulkily, leaning over his sister's shoulder to check the details for himself. 'What's the matter? Do you know her or something?'

'*Yes*,' Olive replied, handing him back the file. 'She

was Grandma Sylvie's lawyer. She's the one who told me about the Memoriser in the first place. She was here, in Grandma Sylvie's house, just two weeks ago.'

At once the annoyed look on Frankie's face vanished and was replaced by one of shock. 'And Grandma thought she might be the mole!'

'Apparently so,' said Olive, her eyes greedily scanning the lines of information beneath the photograph. 'Grandma clearly didn't trust her, anyway. It says that she hasn't always been as discreet as she should have been – that she's known in the world of espionage these days as something of a gossip.'

'Could *she* have stolen the Memoriser? Did she have the *opportunity*?' Frankie whispered, looking around the basement as if worried they'd be overheard.

Olive considered this, then frowned. 'Well, she knew I had it, because she was the one who told me about it. So I suppose she could have come back and taken it . . . but why would she have bothered giving it to me if she was going to have to steal it back? She could have just got rid of the Memoriser in the first place – to stop us working out her secret.' Olive shifted her weight thoughtfully. 'Then again,' she continued, 'the dossier does say that Ms Lowry is very well connected in the spy world. It says she works as a lawyer for all the top spies. So, she certainly had *means* – she might have learned all kinds of skills from years of working with them. And there's a *motive* too – she could have been selling the secrets to her other clients. She might have given the Memoriser to me initially to put us off her scent, and then come back and stolen it later.'

Frankie considered this for a moment. 'OK,' he said slowly as if making a mental note, 'so we can't rule her out as a suspect just yet. We'd better see who's next.'

Olive peered over his shoulder as Frankie opened the next folder.

AGENT NATASHA NEST

This time, staring out at them from a small photograph was a woman with curly red-brown hair and bright grey eyes. She had a clever-looking face with a short, up-turned nose. She was wearing a mustard-yellow turtle-neck jumper beneath a brown chequered blazer and she smiled at the camera in a shy kind of way. If she were a season, thought Olive, taking in her clothes and appearance, she would definitely have been autumn. If she'd been a building, she'd have been a library. And had she been an animal, there was no doubt she'd have been a dormouse.

'This lady's a spy, like Grandma was,' said Frankie.

'It says here,' said Olive, 'that she's had a stellar career within the British Intelligence Service. She was inspired to become a spy by her mother, who was one of the most esteemed espionage agents of her generation. After leaving school, Agent Nest lived in France for several years before joining the British Intelligence Service. She speaks seven languages. *And* she's good at computer hacking and surveillance. I bet those skills would come in very handy for a mole like Shadow. That counts as *means* for sure. Not sure about *motive* or *opportunity* though.'

'Apparently she's good at origami too,' added Frankie, sounding impressed. 'Although maybe that's not quite as useful as the surveillance bit.'

Olive took the folder and placed it carefully next to the other one, so both pictures were facing upwards. 'Two to go,' she said. 'Let's see who we have next.'

Frankie did the honours and opened the third dossier.

PROFESSOR LACHLAN THORN

The photograph inside showed a slim young man with a long neck, large ears and a goatee beard. In the photograph, he was wearing a loose-fitting black T-shirt and was smiling eagerly at the camera.

He had dark curly hair piled high on his head and pale white skin.

Frankie read out his name. 'Looks like he's a scientist of some kind.'

'It says he was born in Edinburgh . . .' read out Olive, 'that he was a child prodigy who went to university at fifteen years old to study neuroscience . . .' (Frankie interjected with an impressed 'oooh' noise at this) '. . . he won some kind of international science prize . . . then he dropped out before he graduated and . . . ah-ha!' Olive said breathily as she came to the last line. What she had read sent an electric jolt right through her body.

'What?' pressed Frankie, wanting to be let in on whatever realisation Olive had just come to.

'Ms Lowry told me that the Memoriser was made by a company called FORGET ME NOT INC. And it says here that Professor Lachlan Thorn is the founder of that exact company!' Olive was triumphant for a moment, then her shoulders sank. 'But . . . I don't know really what that means . . .' she said uncertainly. 'It can't be a coincidence though, can it?'

Frankie was reading the file more carefully now. 'Look, here,' he said, pointing at the dossier, 'it says he used to work for British Intelligence.' He prodded the line on the folder. 'He was the head of scientific research and development, the youngest person to have ever had that role. But then he suddenly left espionage about thirteen years ago. His final mission was called Operation Beehive. It doesn't say why he left, though' Frankie paused thoughtfully, before brightening. 'Oh, that's nice. Says he has two pet huskies called Jekyll and Hyde. I wish Mum would let *us* get a dog.'

Olive was feeling a little overwhelmed. She began to pace across the basement's concrete floor, trying her best to organise her racing thoughts. 'Why would Grandma leave her memories to us if she suspected that the founder of the company that invented the Memoriser had something to do with Shadow?'

'I'm not sure . . .' said Frankie, 'but it sounds like this Professor Thorn had all three: means, motive and opportunity. He was once a skilled spy – so he had the *means*. If he left the agency suddenly it sounds like there might have been a falling-out or something – that might be *motive*. And since he owns the Forget Me Not company, he definitely knew about the Memoriser – that's *opportunity*.' Frankie ticked the things off his fingers one by one, and then chucked the folder on to the table. He reached down for the next – and last –

dossier. 'Moving on to our final contender, we have . . .' He opened the cover theatrically.

AGENT HOWARD SWEET

He held up the folder to show Olive the photograph inside. It showed a man with a full head of neatly combed greyish hair who looked to be in his eighties. His cheeks were drawn in and his chin high, which made him seem either very proud or like he was sucking a sour sweet – depending on the angle you looked at it from.

'He's about the same age as Grandma Sylvie.' Olive stared down at his face. His wrinkled, liver-spotted skin contrasted with the youthful sharpness of his eyes. 'And he was an agent too.' Olive continued reading through the profile carefully. 'Oh look, Grandma's added a few extra notes here. She says they did their agent training together at the same time. And she's written the word *stubborn* and underlined it three times. She's also added *always thinks he's right*.'

Frankie's eyes narrowed. 'That sounds a little suspicious to me, like he and Grandma didn't get on. And he was a spy. That's *means* and maybe even *motive* right there.'

'It does sound suspicious,' agreed Olive, before sighing. 'The problem is, if you ask me there's

something a bit suspicious about *all* of these people.'
The folders lay open across the desk, the four suspects
staring up at the siblings from their photographs. 'Any
one of them could be Shadow.'

Frankie sighed too. 'It would be a lot easier to
work it all out if we had the Memoriser to help us.'

Olive looked at him. 'And that's *exactly* what the
person who stole the Memoriser knew! They wanted
to cover their tracks . . . to stop us working out who
they are. We can't let that happen.'

'But we need more clues!' Frankie replied hopelessly.
'We've no idea which one of these is Shadow.'

'You're right,' agreed Olive. 'But we do know
*something* about Shadow – we know that they're also
the person who stole the Memoriser. So if we find
who the thief is, we find Shadow.'

'How do we do that?' asked Frankie, looking up at
his sister.

Olive studied the folders carefully with narrowed
eyes. 'I think I know where we need to start.' She
prodded the photo in the first folder of the woman
with silver hair and purple lipstick.

'Ms Lowry?' asked Frankie.

'That's right.' Olive nodded. 'She's the one who
told me about it, after all, and she gave me this, so I

know exactly where to find her.' Olive reached into her pocket and produced Ms Lowry's card. Her address was written in small letters along the bottom. Along with the card, a key came tumbling out of Olive's pocket. She looked at it for a moment, deep in thought. Then she turned to her brother, a smile spreading across her face.

'Now all we need to do is work out how we get there . . .' With a glint in her eye, she held up the shiny silver key, the second of the two keys she'd found attached to James's collar. 'Luckily for you, I have a plan. And something tells me that you're going to like it.'

\*

With one hand, Olive held the dossiers. With the other she directed the silver lightning-bolt key at the car and pressed the button. The second she did, the car doors unlocked with a *click*. The siblings turned and stared at one another open-mouthed.

'I can't believe Grandma left us the key!' he said. 'This is the kind of car *famous* people drive.'

'*Good afternoon, Ms Jones.*' A pleasant robotic voice spoke suddenly, making both the children jump.

'*Where would you like to travel to today?*'

Frankie looked as if his eyes might bulge out of their sockets.

'It thinks we're Grandma,' Olive whispered to her brother. She cleared her throat. 'Hello,' she said, feeling pretty foolish for talking to a car. 'Please can we go to –' she checked the card Ms Lowry had given her – 'number 17, Lavender Hill.'

'Certainly,' came the reply from the car. A second later, the back doors glided upwards like the wings of a bird. 'Please watch your step.'

There was a moment when neither of the children moved. 'We're . . . we're really doing this, then,' said Frankie eventually, the nerves causing his voice to shake slightly. His backpack was crammed with all the gadgets they'd found earlier in the cabinet, including the disguises and the explosive football and the GPS tracker pistol. Olive had suggested they pack them so they'd be prepared for anything.

'Looks like it,' Olive replied in the most reassuring voice she could muster. Then, before either of them could change their minds, Olive climbed inside the car, sliding on to a curved velvet sofa, one of two that were facing each other. The body of the car was egg-shaped and made of dark, translucent glass with a floor of thick silver carpet. There was no driver's seat or steering wheel in sight.

'Please make yourself comfortable, Ms Jones,' came the robotic voice of the car. 'Help yourself to refreshments. The journey will take approximately twenty-two minutes.' A table in between the two sofas opened up, revealing a hidden store of drinks and food.

'The car has *snacks*!' cried Frankie excitedly as he clambered on to the seat beside his sister, all trace of nerves vanished. 'And did you hear what it said? We can help ourselves!'

As soon as Frankie was seated, the car doors swooped shut. There was a gentle hum as the engine started. Through the dark glass, they could just make out the movement of a hidden garage door in front of them lifting.

'Here we go,' said Olive. 'Better sit back.'

A moment later the car began to glide gently forward. They entered a narrow cylindrical tunnel with concrete walls illuminated by neon blue lights. The slope was gentle at first but soon became steeper, sending the children sliding backwards in their seats.

'Hold on tight,' called Olive to her brother, fearing that any moment they might suddenly accelerate as if riding a rollercoaster. Then up ahead they saw a flicker of daylight. Not long after, the slope flattened, and the car emerged into the bright afternoon sunshine.

When Olive looked back, the gate had already closed behind them. To her surprise, the opening to the tunnel was situated within the overgrown bushes at the end of her grandmother's garden. These bushes marked the boundary between Grandma Sylvie's property and a car park for a doctor's surgery on the other side. The tunnel's rusted door was graffitied and partly hidden by leaves and crawling ivy. It was something nobody would look twice at, which must have been exactly what Grandma Sylvie counted on.

'Did you know that was there?' asked Frankie.

'Not a clue,' Olive replied, shaking her head. Her grandmother had kept more secrets than she thought one person ever could.

The car shot across the empty car park and out on to the street.

'So what are we going to do when we get there?' Frankie asked, helping himself to a muffin from the snacks compartment.

Olive took a moment to think. 'We'll tell Ms Lowry about the Memoriser being stolen and she how she reacts,' she said at last. 'Then we'll ask her what she knows about Shadow – see if she looks guilty when we mention the name.'

'Got it,' Frankie replied, staring out the window. As he often did when lost in his thoughts, he began humming softly to himself. Olive could tell he was processing everything that had happened in the last hour or so. It was a lot to take in at once. She was relieved when he didn't ask her any more questions. Truth be told, she wasn't really sure what to do when they got there. There was a chance – a high chance – that this plan was a terrible one, that either they'd learn nothing useful, or worse – if Ms Lowry was the mole – that they'd end up in danger.

But she didn't say any of this out loud. As they sped towards Ms Lowry's office – towards the unknown, towards possible danger – Olive didn't want her brother to know quite how nervous she felt.

# CHAPTER SEVEN

## Ms Lowry's Office

Ms Lowry's office was situated in a townhouse on the main high street of their suburban town. It was a slim building, four storeys high and squeezed within a line of other pastel-coloured townhouses in shades of pink and green and blue. The building reminded Olive of the woman herself – tall, elegant, with an air of grandness, its paintwork as colourful as Ms Lowry's purple lipstick.

As they approached the front door, a silver sign which read 'Lowry Legal Services' let them know they were in the right place. Olive shared a look with her brother as if to say *here we go*, before pressing the doorbell down firmly. They waited a moment. When nothing happened, she pressed again.

'Maybe it's broken,' said Frankie. 'Do you think

we should knock instead?'

'Worth a try.' She raised her fist and gave a firm knock. The wooden door gave way beneath her knuckles and swung slowly open.

Olive made a face to her brother and shrugged. 'I guess we're in.'

Inside, they found themselves at the bottom of a steep staircase. Climbing the creaky wooden steps, they soon arrived in a small waiting room with a scattering of seats and paintings of lavender fields hung on walls decorated with stripy purple wallpaper. In the corner was an empty reception desk. It had the eerie feeling of somewhere that's been abandoned, like a disused amusement park.

Olive and Frankie stood side by side, unsure what to do next. The place was quiet, except for the occasional creak of a pipe and the ticking of a large clock on the wall behind the reception desk.

'Doesn't seem like anybody's here,' Olive said uncertainly. Then, in a louder voice, she called, 'Hello, Ms Lowry?'

Frankie looked nervous. 'Maybe she's gone home for the day?' he said hopefully.

'It *is* past five.' Olive looked up at the clock. It was hard to believe how much had happened since she'd left school that afternoon. 'But I think you'd still expect somebody to be here, especially seeing as the front door was unlocked.'

To the left-hand side of the desk was a closed door marked with the words 'Office of Ms Edith Lowry'.

'She must be in here,' said Olive in a hushed voice, and, steeling herself, she knocked firmly on the door.

When there was no answer, Olive took hold of the door handle, twisted and pushed. 'Excuse me, Ms Lowry,' she called as she gently nudged the door open. 'Are you there?'

The children stopped in the doorway. They were looking at a wide room with large windows that overlooked the street below. Like the reception area, it had stripy purple wallpaper and dark wooden furniture. The air smelled faintly of lavender. There were shelves of legal books across one wall and a fireplace on another. It looked like the sort of office you'd expect a lawyer to have, only the desk was littered with scattered papers that appeared to have been thrown around in a hurry, and a potted plant that had been knocked over, its soil spilling out on to the desk. The drawers of the filing cabinets beside the desk were open too, and empty, as if they'd been cleared out in a rush.

Olive looked uncertainly at her brother. 'She's gone.'

'And in a hurry too,' he replied. 'She didn't even take the time to lock the front door.'

Disappointment and confusion churned like cement in Olive's belly. It seemed they'd lost their best lead. She cast her mind back over their meeting two weeks before. 'Ms Lowry was clear that if I had any problems, I'd be able to find her here. It didn't seem like she was planning to go anywhere.'

'Let me get this right.' Frankie crossed his arms. 'Earlier this afternoon the Memoriser was stolen, and around the same time Ms Lowry seems to have cleared out her office and disappeared? If you ask me that's *very* suspicious. Perhaps – having covered her tracks by making it *seem* like she'd given you the Memoriser willingly – she then took the *opportunity* to steal it back and run away before we could work out what she'd done?'

'It is suspicious,' agreed Olive, impressed by her brother's reasoning. 'It's *very* suspicious.' Reaching into Frankie's backpack, she rifled through the four dossiers until she came to the one for Ms Lowry. Then she walked over to the cleared desk and brushed away some soil from the upended plant. Placing the open dossier on the desk, she read through the profile again.

'It says that she's a workaholic who hardly ever takes holidays. And that she's known for being very neat and tidy . . .' Olive trailed off and considered the messy scene before them.

Frankie laughed, picking up a banana peel which had spilled out of a knocked-over bin on to the floor. 'Even tidy people have messy days . . . but this is pushing it. It makes *your* bedroom look spotless!'

'Whatever this looks like,' she said, choosing to ignore her brother's last comment, 'we can't jump to conclusions.'

Another scenario – a horrible one – had occurred to Olive. '*Maybe* she ran away. *Or* . . . maybe Ms Lowry was *kidnapped* – by Shadow. She might have been forced to tell them about the whereabouts of the Memoriser!'

Frankie's eyes grew wide, and Olive was aware once again of the danger their grandmother had led them into. If Shadow were capable of kidnapping Ms Lowry, they could be capable of much worse too.

Olive didn't like to think of Ms Lowry being in that kind of trouble, even if her grandmother had considered her to be a suspect. When they'd met a fortnight before, Ms Lowry had been prickly – even irritable – but she hadn't been unkind. She was also the only person Olive had ever met who had known the *real* Grandma Sylvie. It seemed that every time Olive discovered a connection to her grandmother it wasn't long before it was torn away from her. First the memories, and now Ms Lowry.

'Well,' she said finally, 'we might not be able to get answers from Ms Lowry herself. But we can still search her office for clues.'

Frankie agreed. Gingerly at first, he set about searching through the mess of papers on Ms Lowry's desk while Olive yanked open the drawers and checked the filing cabinet. 'Found anything?' she asked, having confirmed the drawers were indeed all empty.

Frankie shrugged. 'Nothing that seems connected to Grandma Sylvie or any of the suspects. Just lots of boring paperwork. Remind me to *never* become a lawyer.'

Olive sighed. 'There has to be *something* . . .'

With nowhere else to look, she lowered herself to her knees and crawled across the purple carpet, looking under the cabinets and the chair. A moment later, having started to feel a little silly, she saw it – something was lodged underneath the desk.

'I think there's something here!' she exclaimed. 'But I need something long and flat to get it out.'

'Umm –' Frankie rifled through the papers on the desk – 'how about a ruler?' he said, holding one up.

Olive took it from him and slid it under the wooden belly of the desk. Shimmying the ruler towards the object, Olive managed to knock it out into the open. It was then she saw exactly what they'd discovered: a small notebook with a purple leather cover.

'It looks like a diary. It must have got knocked under here by mistake . . . or maybe it's a *secret* diary and this is where Ms Lowry hides it?'

'Maybe! I keep mine hidden under my bed.' Suddenly Frankie looked embarrassed. 'But pretend you didn't hear that.'

Olive ran her hand over the purple leather. A silver ribbon was tucked between two pages about halfway through the book. Opening it to the bookmarked page, Olive saw that it was indeed a diary. Her heart did a somersault in her chest.

'Look . . . look at this!' she said excitedly, reading it through. 'There's an entry from today. The letters "*H.S.*" Underlined twice. And below that, an address, and a time. Ten o'clock.'

'H.S.,' repeated Frankie. 'Somebody's initials, maybe?'

'Must be . . . oh!' cried Olive, suddenly

remembering. She went over to the four grey folders on the desk, flicking through them until she came to the one she needed. 'Howard Sweet!' she announced triumphantly. She opened the file and prodded the photograph of the elderly man. He stared coolly back with a look of disapproval. He appeared to Olive every bit as stubborn as Grandma Sylvie had described in the dossier.

'Do you think he was one of Ms Lowry's clients too, like Grandma Sylvie was?' asked Frankie.

'Maybe,' replied Olive. 'It certainly can't be a coincidence that two of the main suspects met the very morning the Memoriser was stolen. In any case, we definitely need to talk to Howard Sweet. Let's jump in Grandma's car and head to this address right away!'

Frankie nodded excitedly and Olive couldn't help but grin. 'We've found a clue all by ourselves! What would Grandma Sylvie say if she could see us? Do you think she'd be proud?'

'Not as proud as when I solved her chess clue . . .' Frankie's face broke into a wry smile, and Olive rolled her eyes. 'But yeah, she definitely would be. Although, she'd probably also tell us to get a move on. Mum will be home from work soon.'

With their plan decided, Olive and Frankie dashed

out of Ms Lowry's office, taking the diary with them. Olive checked the clock on the wall as they passed through the reception area on the way out. It was now half past five. Their mother was due home in thirty minutes. Frankie was right; they needed to get on the road, and fast.

They rushed down the stairs and out the door. Olive had been worried when they'd left the car that it might be stolen or damaged. But the car was right where they'd left it, its glossy paintwork shining in the late afternoon sun. However, that wasn't all that was waiting for them. Leaning up against the car was a woman with curly red-brown hair. The children took a few tentative steps towards her and the woman straightened and smiled.

'Olive, Frankie. I was hoping I would meet you both soon.'

The children had studied the photographs in the folders long enough to recognise the woman at once. It wasn't *exactly* the same mustard-yellow turtleneck or the same chequered blazer, but it was very much like the outfit she'd been wearing in the picture they'd seen in the dossier, except the real-life version was shabbier, with moth holes all over, and mismatched patches of fabric sewn haphazardly at the elbows. Her only jewellery was a small silver necklace resting above her jumper. There was nothing of the glamour Olive had pictured when she'd imagined a spy. The woman had a bookish sort of look, the kind of person you might easily overlook in a busy room. She was barely taller than the children with alert grey eyes and curly red-brown hair that bounced as she spoke.

'You won't know me, but my name is Natasha.' Her voice was quiet, so that Olive had to strain to hear her. 'I was a friend of your grandmother's. I'm terribly sorry for your loss.'

'Agent Natasha Nest,' replied Olive coolly. 'We know who you are.'

Agent Nest's thin lips twitched into a smile. 'Oh, you do? I'm glad to hear it.'

'Why . . . are you here?' managed Frankie, surprising Olive with his boldness. He was usually shy around strangers. 'How did you find us?'

'I have a knack for finding people when I need to.'

This startled Olive, but she tried not to let her face show it. It was very strange indeed to be meeting a real-life spy. 'You saved us a job.' She tried her best to sound casual. 'Because we want to speak to you too.'

A look, which might have been surprise, passed across Agent Nest's round face, but it vanished a moment later. 'In that case, how about we talk over a cup of tea, and possibly a slice of cake too?' she said gently. 'The café across the road makes the best carrot cake around.'

Frankie gave Olive a nervous glance. 'Our mum is expecting us home any minute,' Olive replied cautiously.

'It won't take long. Ten minutes at most. But it's important we talk.' Agent Nest leaned forward and lowered her already soft voice. 'It's about Mission Shadow.'

# CHAPTER EIGHT

## Trust Has to Go Both Ways

The café had gingham tablecloths and pictures of scones dancing with pots of jam on the walls. It seemed to Olive to be a funny place to hold a meeting with a spy. There was a counter with an array of cakes, cookies and muffins under glass cloches. Sunlight streamed through the front window, warming the sugary air. A bell rang as the party of three entered and a waitress appeared to greet them. She smiled at Agent Natasha Nest before rushing to wipe down a table beside the window. When the table was ready, Olive and her brother took seats beside one another and across from the agent, as if they were police officers preparing to interview their suspect.

'We'd like three slices of carrot cake, please,' Agent Nest said pleasantly to the waitress, tucking a strand of curly red-brown hair behind her ear. 'And a large pot of tea.'

'I'll bring the three biggest slices we have,' she replied with kind twinkly eyes, before disappearing.

As soon as the waitress was out of earshot, Agent Nest began. 'I'm thrilled to meet you both. I've heard lots about you over the years. Your grandmother thought so much of you.' The children shared a look. Despite what they'd read in her letters, they still found it hard to believe that their grandmother had cared for them. And even harder to believe she would have told other people about it. Agent Nest, undeterred, continued warmly. 'And you seem to know a bit about me too. Is that right?'

'We know that you're a spy,' said Olive, 'and that your mother was a spy too.'

'Quite so,' Agent Nest replied softly. 'As a rule, of course, I never tell civilians the truth about what I do for a living. As far as the public knows, I've worked for twenty years as a translator for the United Nations. It helps to explain the constant travelling, you see. But I can tell there's little point in lying to you two! I've known Sylvie since I was a child. She was best friends with my late mother. As a colleague, we worked together for years.' She touched the necklace around her neck absent-mindedly. 'Oh, I can't tell you how honoured I was to work with your grandmother . . . the legendary Sylvie Jones.'

At this last comment, Olive struggled to hold her tongue. Sitting across from somebody who'd known their grandmother like that – who'd worked as a spy alongside her – was difficult. She had to fight the urge to blurt out questions about her life. *Wait until you've completed Mission Shadow*, Olive reminded herself. Then she'd be free to find out everything she could about her grandmother. For now, she had to focus on the job at hand.

Olive couldn't afford to let her guard down either. As a contender for Shadow, Agent Nest was a good one. She was still an active spy for a start. She'd spent years working closely with Grandma Sylvie, giving her access to plenty of secret information. Now it turned out that she knew about Mission Shadow, even though Grandma Sylvie claimed to have kept it top secret. It occurred to Olive that Agent Nest might have known about the mission precisely because *she* was Shadow. Yet, if that were the case, Olive had no clue what Agent Nest's motive might have been. She could have been driven by greed, of course. Shadow would have become very rich over so many years. And yet with her moth-eaten clothing, Agent Nest didn't seem like a particularly wealthy person. Still, Grandma Sylvie had said it was likely about more than money. As she'd written in her letter: *the motive had to be personal.*

With all this in the back of her mind, Olive asked something that had been troubling her since she'd first set eyes on Agent Nest. 'How exactly did you find us here?' Her eyes narrowed. 'Have you been following us?'

Agent Nest looked confused. 'Following you? Of course not. I've spent the day right here in this café, watching Edith Lowry's office. It's not the most exciting assignment I've ever had, that's for sure.' She was pulling at a loose thread in the sleeve of her chequered jacket. 'But at least there's plenty of tea. Twenty-five different types to be exact.'

'Watching her office,' said Frankie, his nose scrunched. 'What for?'

'It's called surveillance,' replied Agent Nest. 'There are rumours in the British Intelligence Service that Ms Edith Lowry has something to do with high-level information leaks. My mission is to see whether those rumours are true.'

Frankie looked across at Olive. 'Our grandma thought she might be untrustworthy, too!'

'Have you really been here *all* day?' Olive asked bluntly, ignoring Frankie. 'You've not left once?' If Agent Nest was Shadow, she'd have good reason to make them believe Ms Lowry was untrustworthy. And Olive wouldn't fall for it like her brother had, at least not yet. First, she needed to find out if what she'd said about being here all day was the truth. After all, if it was true, then Agent Nest couldn't have stolen the Memoriser earlier that afternoon. This gave her a strong alibi. *If* she was telling the truth.

'Have I left?' Agent Nest sighed. 'Not once. I've been here since first thing this morning. And so far, it's been a total waste of time. Though it's been worth it to have run into you two.'

'Have you seen any sign of Ms Lowry?' asked Olive. 'Has anyone else come or gone?'

'I saw her leave her office at nine o'clock this morning,' replied Agent Nest. 'She hasn't been back since. And nobody else has shown up all day, until you two arrived, that is.'

Olive considered this. It seemed unlikely that Ms Lowry had been kidnapped by Shadow, if she was seen leaving on time for her meeting with Howard Sweet. Watching Agent Nest across the table, Olive's head was full of facts from the agent's file. That for instance she could play piano, speak seven languages and was expert in several kinds of martials arts. It was hard to reconcile this impressive collection of skills with the quiet, somewhat unremarkable person sitting in front of her.

A moment later, the waitress reappeared balancing a tray with cups, a teapot and three enormous slices of thickly iced carrot cake. 'Thank you ever so much,' said Agent Nest when everything was set down on the table.

The waitress beamed, returning to the counter. 'Now,' said the spy, adding a dash of milk to the three cups and motioning to Olive and Frankie to help themselves to cake, 'I know you don't have much time, so let's get down to business. There's a matter I'd like to discuss with you. A serious matter, I'm afraid to say.'

Olive swallowed a mouthful of cake, before setting down her fork. 'If it's about Mission Shadow,' she said firmly, 'then we have some questions for you too. Like how exactly you came to know about it.'

Agent Nest took a sip of tea before starting. 'Not long before your grandmother's death, she confided in me about her problems with a mole code-named *Shadow*.'

Frankie sat forward in his chair, clearly hanging on the agent's every word. Olive was intrigued too but tried to keep a little more reserved.

'Your grandmother told me,' continued Agent Nest, lowering her quiet voice, 'that somebody from within the Service was stealing secrets from her and selling them to some rather bad people. Sylvie kept her cards close to her chest, like any good spy would. But I know how dangerous she considered this person – this *mole* in the British Intelligence Service – to be.'

Olive tried to make her face unreadable. She needed to keep her cards just as close to her chest as Grandma Sylvie had kept her own. 'Did she tell you who she thought might be stealing the secrets?' she asked.

Agent Nest shook her head sadly, sheltering her teacup in her hands. 'She never got the chance. And I'm afraid to say, ever since her death terrible rumours have started to circulate. Those rumours say that it was in fact Sylvie herself who was selling secrets, with the help of Ms Lowry. The chief of the intelligence service – a man called Sir Bobbie Eden – is convinced of it.'

'No!' Olive was appalled. 'It *wasn't* Grandma Sylvie. She was trying to find out who the culprit was. She was trying to stop them!'

Agent Nest's grey eyes widened. '*I* know that. Believe me I do. But without proof, I can't do anything about it. The damage to your grandmother's reputation has already been catastrophic. The only way we can fix that is by exposing the real Shadow.'

Frankie leaned forward excitedly. 'That's exactly what *we're* trying to do, too.'

Agent Nest sat back. 'I can see now why your grandmother spoke so highly of you both.'

'She did?' Frankie asked eagerly. Olive, meanwhile, had started to feel clammy all over, thinking about her grandmother being given the blame for what Shadow had done. It wasn't fair. It wasn't right. She couldn't let it happen. She *wouldn't*.

Olive glanced at Frankie, who was glowing with pride. Agent Nest stared at the children seriously, before continuing. 'I've been trying to work out how to clear her name. It occurred to me that if Sylvie would have told anyone else about Shadow, it would have been you two. I can see now that I was right. Tell me, was there anything she told you . . . or perhaps left behind that might help us identify the real Shadow?'

Olive faltered, reeling from everything she'd just learned. Frankie stared up at her expectantly. It was clear he wanted them to tell Agent Nest everything.

Her brother had always been quick to trust others, unlike Olive, who was known for harbouring suspicions about the postman or her supply teachers. Being trusting was a very good quality to have, of course, and Olive wouldn't change her brother for anything. But it wasn't going to help them now. If television had taught her anything, it was that in the world of espionage, trusting the wrong person could be fatal.

Olive thought back to Grandma Sylvie's letters. *Only accept help from those you trust with your life*, she'd written. Agent Nest didn't qualify. But, then again, if Grandma Sylvie had trusted Agent Nest enough to tell her about Mission Shadow, perhaps they should too. Not for the first time, Olive wished her grandmother was there to ask for advice. 'You might be right that Grandma Sylvie confided in us,' she said finally. 'But . . . how can we be sure that we can trust *you*?'

'The thing I've learned about trust, Olive, from many years in the business, is that it has to go both ways. We have to trust each other.' She watched Olive for a moment, a searching look in her careful eyes, making Olive feel like she was being x-rayed. 'Tell me, what's your middle name?'

Olive was thrown. She didn't know what her middle name had to do with anything. 'It's . . . Violet.'

'Can you guess what my mother's name was?' Olive's mouth open and closed. 'When you were born,' continued Agent Nest, 'your father and mother wanted your middle name to be Sylvie. Your grandmother asked them to choose Violet, instead. She wanted to honour my mother and their long friendship.' She paused, allowing her words to sink in. Her hand went to her silver necklace. She unclasped the chain and lifted it above her head before passing it over to Olive. 'Open the locket,' she directed, and Olive did as she was told. Inside she found a faded photograph. It was of two young women standing next to each other and smiling. Olive instantly recognised one of the women as her grandmother. The other looked very much like Agent Nest, with short curly red hair. It had to be Violet Nest. Looking over his sister's shoulder, Frankie exhaled slowly.

'So, Olive *Violet* Jones,' continued Agent Nest, 'you can trust me.'

After a moment, Olive handed back the necklace. While Agent Nest put it back on, Olive took a shaky sip of her tea. She did *want* to trust Agent Nest. She wanted to hear more about dangerous missions she'd completed with Grandma Sylvie. She wanted to know more about the stranger who she'd apparently been named after and yet never been told about before. Olive had missed so much by not getting to know her grandmother. Agent Nest could help her to fill in those gaps, as well as helping them to complete Mission Shadow. If only Olive could allow herself to trust her.

But Olive hadn't forgotten her promise not to tell anyone about the Memoriser. True, she'd broken it to confide in Frankie, but she'd a feeling that was what her grandmother intended all along. She wasn't about to tell one of Grandma's prime suspects about it. To get Agent Nest's help, however, she sensed that she'd better share *something* with her. The trick would be not giving away too much.

Olive gave Frankie a look, which she hoped he'd understand meant *follow my lead*. Then she took a deep breath. There was no taking back what she was about to say. 'Grandma Sylvie wanted us to help her catch Shadow. And she left us some information to help us do that. That's why we came to Ms Lowry's office this afternoon. To see what *she* knew about all of this.'

Agent Nest nodded encouragingly. 'So we're here

for the same reason. Did you find anything when you searched her office?'

'Well . . . yes and no,' said Olive. 'Ms Lowry wasn't there, as you know, but we found something else.' Olive slid the notebook across the table. 'There's an entry in the diary for this morning, which suggests that Ms Lowry went to meet a spy called Howard Sweet. And it says where.'

'I see.' Agent Nest frowned as she picked up the diary and checked the latest entry. 'What was Howard Sweet doing meeting your grandmother's lawyer this morning?'

'We think they were planning to steal—' began Frankie, but Olive shot him a look of thunder that quietened him at once. To Olive's relief, Agent Nest was still carefully examining the notebook and hadn't seemed to notice the exchange.

'We believe that Howard met Ms Lowry,' Olive began calmly, 'because she was helping him steal secrets from Grandma. We think he might be Shadow.' She chose her words carefully, so as not to give anything away about the existence of the Memoriser.

'That fits with my own suspicions,' Agent Nest replied gravely, finally looking up. 'Howard Sweet and your grandmother had a rocky relationship. They were always falling out. Sometimes they stopped speaking for years at a time. He was the first person I thought of when she told me about Shadow. He must also be the one trying to frame Sylvie, to shift the blame to her.'

'Have you questioned him?' asked Olive.

'I've tried. He suddenly retired from the Service not long after your grandmother died and has gone into hiding. I've spent a couple of weeks trying to track him down without any luck. But this diary . . .' She raised her eyebrows, looking genuinely impressed. '. . . it's the first clue I've had in weeks.'

'What are we waiting for, then? Let's go now.' Olive pushed back her chair with a scrape. It suddenly felt like a terrible waste of time to be sitting in a café enjoying tea and cake when they should be out there finding Howard Sweet and clearing their grandmother's name.

'Hold your horses, Olive,' replied Agent Nest gently. 'You've not even finished your tea.'

Without breaking eye contact, Olive picked up her cup and drained it. This made Agent Nest laugh, and though it wasn't an unkind laugh, it still made Olive prickle with annoyance.

'But we're wasting time!' Olive appealed to her

brother for support, trying her best to keep her temper in control. 'We need to go after Howard Sweet *right now.*'

Frankie, who was the only one to have finished his huge slice of cake, looked across at Olive anxiously. 'I don't know if that's a good . . .' was all he managed before dropping his eyes.

Agent Nest's face was awash with sympathy. 'Olive, I understand how you feel completely.' Olive inwardly scoffed. She hated when people said things like *I understand how you feel*, because they so rarely did. 'You'd both make fine spies,' Agent Nest continued. 'Your grandmother would have been exceptionally proud of your willingness to take this on. But she didn't understand the full extent of this campaign to frame her. It's serious, Olive. We don't have a lot of time. Your grandmother's reputation is at stake. And I need to keep you two safe too. Howard Sweet is a dangerous man. Sylvie wouldn't have wanted you to be in that kind of danger.' She signalled to the waitress for the bill. 'Take your grandmother's car and go home. Your mother will be worrying about you. Leave the rest to me for now.'

'But we know what we're doing, don't we, Frankie?' Olive was unable to hide the hurt in her voice. Agent

Nest clearly didn't think they were up to the job. 'We've come this far . . .'

'The world of espionage isn't a place for children.' Agent Nest took a moment to consider the notebook, before closing it and sliding it into her jacket pocket. 'I'll find Howard Sweet and Edith Lowry and, if our suspicions are right, I'll make sure they both face justice. You have my word. But for now, I need to protect you both. It's what your grandmother would have wanted. As soon as everything is taken care of, I promise I'll find you again and tell you everything that's happened. I have so many stories to share with you about your remarkable grandmother.'

Agent Nest smiled so warmly at Olive that, to her embarrassment, Olive felt tears pricking her eyes. All she ever wanted was to know her grandmother, for her grandmother to be proud of her.

A saucer appeared containing the bill. Agent Nest produced a bank note from inside her jacket and placed it carefully on the table. 'Thank you both again. I couldn't have done this without you. Finding Howard's address like this could have broken the case for us. You've done an incredible job.' She rose from her seat. 'Now, let's get you safely back home.'

Olive opened her mouth to protest once more, but

Agent Nest and her brother were already halfway to the door. It seemed that as far as they were concerned, the matter, like the bill, had just been settled.

And Olive knew it made sense. But she had to be sure first. There was one last thing she needed to check out.

As soon as the door had closed behind her brother and Agent Nest, Olive raced over to the waitress, who was refilling a plate of cookies. 'That lady I was just with . . .' Olive began in a rush. 'How long has she been here?'

The waitress blinked with surprise. 'Oh . . . all day . . . she arrived right after I opened at nine o'clock. Such a nice woman.'

'Are you sure?' Olive pressed, aware that she wasn't being particularly well-mannered. 'It's really important that you are.'

'Absolutely sure. It's been a quiet day. She's sat right there at that table and stared out the window. Ordered about a dozen teas and coffees, oh and a hot choc—'

'Has she left at all?' Olive interrupted.

'Yes . . .' Olive's body went tense with anticipation. 'But only once,' the waitress went on. 'And then she came back with you and your friend.'

Olive's shoulders sank. There was no doubt about it, Agent Nest's alibi was strong. If she'd spent the whole day in the café then she couldn't have also stolen the Memoriser earlier that afternoon. Agent Nest wasn't Shadow. She was an experienced spy. The mission would be in safe hands with her – safer no doubt than with a couple of kids. Olive glumly thanked the waitress (who by this time was starting to look a little sour herself) and walked out of the café, back towards her grandmother's car, towards home.

# CHAPTER NINE

## Leave No Stone Unturned

It was a long, quiet drive home. Olive sat opposite her brother in a stormy silence. Every metre they travelled felt like it was in the wrong direction. She knew it made sense on paper to leave the case with Agent Nest, but somehow it didn't *feel* right. On some level, she was certain that rather than driving back to their house they should have been with Agent Nest setting out to interrogate Howard Sweet.

'We did the right thing, Olive,' said Frankie softly. 'It's gone six o'clock. We'll be in enough trouble as it is.' Frankie spoke in the most consoling voice he could muster. 'Besides, Agent Nest is an experienced spy. She knows exactly what to do. She'll stop Shadow *and* get the Memoriser back. We'll finally be able to watch Grandma Sylvie's memories. That's what we want really, isn't it?'

When you are in a bad mood – the kind of mood where the whole world seems to have turned against you – and somebody comes along with sensible advice, it is almost guaranteed to make your mood even gloomier. Her brother, sensing this was the case, fell quiet for the rest of the journey, not humming so much as a note.

Eventually the car reached their grandmother's basement, passing through the secret entrance in the doctor's car park they had exited earlier. The children rode the armchair back up to their grandmother's living room, one after the other, in stony silence, then left the bungalow, locking the front door behind them.

Arriving home, Olive and Frankie crept on tiptoes down the hallway towards their bedrooms. They hoped that if they could reach their rooms undiscovered, they could convince their mother they'd been there all along. But they hadn't even made it halfway down the hallway when their mother appeared from the kitchen with a look of fury.

'Where have you two been?' she demanded. 'Do you have any idea how worried I was when I got home and neither of you were here?'

Olive froze. In the shock of Mission Shadow being

over, they had completely forgotten to come up with a cover story.

'Chess club ran late,' said Frankie quickly. 'Olive waited for me so we could . . . walk home together.'

Olive blinked. Her brother was usually a terrible liar, but somehow he'd been quick enough to think of a plausible excuse, which was more than she could say for herself. Olive looked at her mother, relieved to see her anger had softened ever so slightly. 'You should have called me,' her mother said, turning to address Olive directly. 'I thought something terrible had happened to you both.'

Olive and Frankie muttered their apologies, guilt churning in their stomachs. For the rest of the evening, both the children were as helpful as they could be, in the hope that it would get them back into their mother's good books. They also hoped it would stop her from asking too many questions. When it came to sitting down to dinner though, neither one was very hungry, partly due to the disappointment of the mission being over, and partly due to having eaten the large slices of carrot cake and treats from the driverless car. Their mother watched suspiciously as her children pushed potatoes and carrots around their plates.

'You're very quiet,' she said eventually.

'I thought you liked it when we were quiet,' replied Frankie. He gave a cheeky grin, the kind that usually let him get away with anything.

'And *I* thought you were cross with us,' added Olive defensively.

'I *do* and I *am*,' their mother agreed, 'but I still want to talk to you. How were your days? Was everything OK at school?'

'Fine,' they both replied, a little too quickly. 'School was boring, as usual,' Olive added, rolling her eyes in the way she usually did at this sort of question and taking a mouthful of carrots, hoping this would help convince her mother that everything was completely normal.

Olive felt her mother's gaze bore into her. But to her surprise, when their mother spoke again, her voice was gentle and concerned.

'It's only been a couple of weeks since the funeral,' she began. 'I know you weren't as close to your grandmother as you might have been. But if either of you would like to talk about your grandmother, and you know . . . about how you're feeling, you can always come to me. You know that, don't you, Olive?'

Olive stabbed a floret of broccoli with her fork, wishing the conversation would end immediately.

'I know, Mum. But I'm fine, really.'

'Are you sure? You've been acting a bit strange these last two weeks,' her mother replied.

'Yes, Mum.' Olive felt hotness creep over her face. Though she wasn't exactly sure why, the concerned gaze of her mother always made her feel a little cross and embarrassed. She would usually rather talk about almost anything else than her emotions, and especially in this moment, when Olive had no choice but to lie.

To her relief, Olive's mother dropped the subject, and Frankie, seeing that Olive was struggling, managed to steer the conversation towards talking about why he loved the theme tune from *Jaws* (which he performed with a broccoli shark as a prop). Olive was grateful for this and used the time to think about everything that had happened. Even if she was off the case, there was surely nothing wrong in thinking over the day's events, making sure it all added up.

In her head, Olive ran over everything she knew so far. Thanks to the diary they'd found in Ms Lowry's office, she knew that Ms Lowry had had planned to meet with Howard Sweet at 10 a.m. Not long after that, the Memoriser was stolen. And at some point during the day, Ms Lowry's office had been left in a terrible mess. A picture formed in Olive's mind of Ms

Lowry meeting Howard Sweet, him asking her about the Memoriser, her telling him that it had been delivered to Olive, and him setting out to steal it, while Ms Lowry decided to clear out her office and disappear so she wouldn't face the consequences of her indiscretion. Did Howard Sweet pay her for this? It must have been a lot for her to decide it was worth leaving town for. Did he get that money from selling Grandma Sylvie's secrets? The evidence so far certainly seemed to point towards Howard Sweet being Shadow.

As for Agent Nest, it seemed impossible that she could have stolen the Memoriser, when she had such a strong alibi. And she had clearly been close to Grandma Sylvie, having known her since she was a child. So she had no opportunity, and no known motive.

All of this seemed to fit together neatly. So why did it make Olive feel so unsatisfied? Something was telling her that there was more to the story than she currently knew. After all, her grandmother had left her *four* dossiers for a reason.

As she finished the last of her potatoes, Olive was reminded of something. Ms Lowry wasn't the *only* person who knew about the Memoriser. There was another suspect who'd certainly known about it –

because they, in fact, had made it. Professor Lachlan Thorn, a former spy turned entrepreneur, and the founder of Forget Me Not Inc. Olive thought back to his file. Might he be involved in some way? Why would their grandmother have given them a dossier on Professor Thorn if she wasn't suspicious of him? They owed it to her to at least talk to him.

By the time dinner had ended, she'd made up her mind.

'Frankie, you'll help me do the washing up, won't you?'

Frankie looked at his sister suspiciously. 'Umm . . . OK.'

With a bemused look on her face, their mother headed to the living room. Frankie followed Olive into the kitchen, carrying stacks of plates and cutlery. They left the washing up in a pile beside the sink and Olive turned on both taps, hoping the noise of the running water would cover their voices.

'Listen, Frankie,' she whispered excitedly, 'it's not over yet. We have to continue our investigation.'

Frankie's shoulders sank. 'Olive, come on . . .'

'Leave no stone unturned, remember? That's what Grandma wrote in her letter. We need to pay a visit to the place the Memoriser was made . . . we need to go to Forget Me Not Inc.'

Now Frankie looked afraid. 'But Agent Nest said—'

'I know what she said,' Olive snapped. 'But *we* said we'd interview all the suspects. We owe it to Grandma. We know about the other three suspects, I've met two of them myself, and Agent Nest is dealing with the third. Professor Lachlan Thorn is the only one that we know nothing about.'

At that moment, their mother appeared in the doorway. She frowned, seeing the tap running and the dishes untouched. 'There's more to washing dishes than turning on the tap, you know? It takes a bit of soap and scrubbing too.' Olive smiled sheepishly and rushed to turn off the taps. Their mother tutted and walked out of the room again. 'Frankie, it's bedtime for you. Go and brush your teeth, please,' she said over her shoulder.

As soon as she was gone, Olive carried on in a loud whisper. 'Here's the plan. Tomorrow, we'll leave as if we're going to school. Then we'll sneak back into Grandma's house and take the car to Forget Me Not. Even if we don't learn anything new about Mission Shadow from him, we can at least ask for a copy of Grandma's memories.'

Staring up at Olive, Frankie frowned thoughtfully.

'Won't school notice if we don't show up? And how will we even know where to find this professor?'

Olive smiled. Frankie was starting to consider the logistics, which meant she was winning him over. 'I'll sort out school, don't worry. And Grandma Sylvie's car will know how to find Forget Me Not. Trust me – this is the right thing to do. You do trust me, don't you?'

'You know I do – *with my life*.' Frankie smiled and shook his head, before laughing. 'I just don't want it to *actually* get me killed. Speaking of which –' he stifled a yawn – 'I'd better go to bed before Mum comes back and takes care of that for us. Na-night, Olive.'

Olive hugged her brother, celebrating inwardly. 'Sweet dreams,' she said. She gave him what she hoped was a reassuring smile, and as she turned back to the washing up, she thought how nice it was, for once, to have a partner in crime.

*

Lying in bed later that night, Olive was unable to sleep. In her head she went over and over her plan for the following day. After her brother had gone to bed, she'd snuck over to her mother's laptop, tapped in her password (which she'd known for some years was *OliveandFrankie*) and sent an email to the school secretary. In it she'd explained, with the best spelling and grammar she could manage, that she and Frankie had both developed a terrible case of chicken pox. The whole thing had taken less than five minutes and made Olive wonder why she hadn't tried it before. It was only now, as she lay in bed, that worry began to creep into her head. What if the school figured out what she'd done? What if her teacher called her mother to check in? What if the car didn't know how to get to Forget Me Not, or if it did, what if Professor Thorn wasn't there, or wouldn't speak to them? Olive turned over and over, flipping her pillow around and throwing off her duvet. However much she tried, she couldn't settle.

Admitting defeat, Olive sat up in bed, crawled towards the window and drew back the curtain. Across the road, under the light of a streetlamp, she saw her grandmother's bungalow. How many times had she watched Grandma Sylvie walk up to the front door, her shopping in one hand and trolley bag in the other? Why hadn't Olive taken any of those chances to run up to her grandmother? She could have offered her help with carrying her shopping. Even though she knew that Grandma Sylvie had been more than strong enough to carry her own, it still would have been nice to offer. Olive could have tried harder to close the distance between them, no matter how much her grandmother resisted. There were a million things that Olive wanted to talk to Grandma Sylvie about, a million questions she longed to ask her. And now she'd never get the chance.

Well, at least she could help her with this one last thing. Olive decided to stop worrying about *how* she was going to complete Mission Shadow. Now she would focus on the *why*. It was for her grandmother. With this thought firmly in mind, and nothing else, Olive finally drifted into a deep, dreamless sleep.

## CHAPTER TEN

# Forget Me Not

The next morning Olive and Frankie gulped down their breakfast as fast as they could, waved goodbye to their mother at the door like always and set off down the street. When they were completely sure the coast was clear, they doubled back towards their grandmother's bungalow.

Not long after that, they were on their way, sailing down the motorway in the glinting driverless car. As Olive had suspected, the car had known exactly how to get to Forget Me Not. In a matter of minutes, they'd left their small town far behind as the car sped through rolling countryside and quaint villages dotted with smoking chimneys and homely looking pubs.

But when just under an hour later the car announced that they were approaching their destination, Olive had a horrible feeling they were in the wrong place. They had turned on to a remote road set within a forest of pine trees which stretched for miles on either side. Surely a major laboratory wouldn't be located *here*? They seemed to be in the middle of nowhere. Olive was relieved when a moment later they turned a corner and she saw a metallic blue sign which read FORGET ME NOT INC.

Hurtling past the sign, they drove towards a round cabin made of ash-coloured timber with windows looking out into the surrounding trees. The driverless car came to a gentle stop outside and with a *click* the doors unlocked and lifted open. The children stepped out on to hard-packed earth and filled their lungs with cool, pine-fragranced air.

Frankie stretched his legs that were stiff from the long drive and looked around. 'You wouldn't expect to find somewhere like Forget Me Not out here, in the middle of nowhere, would you?'

Olive shook her head and frowned. 'It's so small too. Only a single storey.' They were standing on a path which sloped up to a glass door at the front of the cabin. 'This must be the entrance,' she said. 'Come on, then.'

The glass doors slid open automatically as they

approached. With a nod to Frankie, Olive led them through and into a circular room with pale timber walls and floor. Large windows looked out on to the surrounding forest, and the room was filled with morning light. The high vaulted ceiling was crossed with beams. Beside a wood-burning stove on one side of the room were a couple of wooden chairs and a small table. At the centre of the cabin stood a tall crystal sculpture of a blue flower, which shimmered in the daylight. Otherwise, the room was empty.

'That doesn't really seem like it fits in here, does it?' Frankie nodded towards the sculpture, which was almost twice his height.

'I've seen that flower before,' Olive whispered back. 'It's the same one that was on the Memoriser box. It's called a forget-me-not.'

'*Hello, visitors*,' came a gentle robotic voice, seemingly from nowhere. '*Welcome to Forget Me Not Inc. How can I help you today?*'

'Um . . .' Olive looked around the empty room, confused. 'We'd like to speak with Professor Lachlan Thorn, please,' she said to the air.

'*Please give your reason for visiting Professor Thorn.*'

Olive gave her brother a sideways glance, before

continuing. 'We need to talk to him about a very urgent matter.'

'*The reason for your visit has not been recognised,*' the voice said.

Olive tried again. 'Would you let Professor Thorn know that Sylvie Jones's grandchildren are here to see him? It's about one of his Memorisers.'

'*Your message has been shared.*' There was a pause. '*Please provide your names.*'

'Olive and Frankie Jones.'

There was another long pause. Then, '*Professor Thorn will come up to meet you. Please wait here.*'

The children fidgeted nervously as they waited. Fortunately, they didn't have to wait long. A few minutes later, at the far end of the room, a cylindrical glass lift appeared, rising up through an opening in the wooden floor. The lift door opened, and the man inside it stepped out. The children recognised him at once from his file. He was tall with long, slim legs and the arms and neck to match. The shirt and jeans he wore were casual and loose fitting. His scraggly goatee covered a boyish face. His dark hair was unkempt, as if he'd only recently got out of bed.

'What a surprise,' said Professor Lachlan Thorn, in an accent Olive recognised as Scottish. He was looking at them with round eager eyes and a broad grin. 'Are you really the grandchildren of the legendary Sylvie Jones?'

Olive flushed. Hearing her grandmother described as *the legendary Sylvie Jones* would take some getting used to. 'We are. My name is Olive,' she said, 'and this is Frankie. We're sorry to just turn up like this but—'

'Please don't be sorry,' he replied, waving his hand enthusiastically. 'Your grandmother warned me that you might come to see me. Though I didn't expect you quite as soon as this. In fact, if you had come any earlier, you'd have missed me entirely. I've just returned this morning from a business trip abroad. Excuse my appearance. I never cope well with jet lag.'

Olive noted this fact with interest. If Professor Thorn had only just returned from a trip then he surely couldn't have stolen the Memoriser the day before. She was also surprised to hear that Professor Thorn was expecting them, though perhaps she shouldn't have been. Grandma Sylvie had clearly planned everything with great care.

Professor Thorn's eyes shone with intrigue as he peered down at them. 'You received the Memoriser yesterday, didn't you?' he said. 'And I bet that you're here because you're curious about how it works?'

'We *are* curious, but—'

'Curiosity is such a wonderful thing,' he said, cutting her off. 'Well, Olive and Frankie Jones, though the technology itself is not an easy thing to explain, what I can do is give you a little tour of Forget Me Not. What do you say?'

The professor spoke so enthusiastically that Olive could hardly say no. And anyway, if they asked him lots of questions right away and he figured out why they'd really come – to interrogate him about Mission Shadow – he might tell them to leave. But if they agreed to a tour, Olive could subtly ask the questions she needed to ask along the way. What she wanted to work out was whether Professor Thorn was still somehow connected to the spy world, and whether he held any sort of grudge against Grandma Sylvie – whether, in other words, he had *means* or *motive*. And if she could also find out whether he had really been abroad the previous day when the Memoriser was stolen, then so much the better.

Besides these important reasons, Olive couldn't resist the chance to explore somewhere like Forget Me Not. Ever since Ms Lowry had mentioned its name a fortnight earlier, she'd been desperate to know more about it. She glanced at Frankie, who she knew would be just as curious. He was looking up at Olive hopefully.

'Well don't both say yes at once, will you!' the professor said with a forced laugh. He clearly didn't think his offer was one that any child would have to consider for long.

'Yes, please,' said Olive, quickly getting her thoughts together. 'We'd love to have a tour.'

'Good.' He clapped his hands together. 'In that case, you'd better follow me.' Not wasting any time, Professor Thorn waved the children towards the open doors of the glass lift, which was spacious enough to fit the three of them comfortably. Once they were safely inside, the glass door closed.

'Please give my guests temporary security clearance,' said Professor Thorn into thin air. 'And take us to the laboratory.'

'*Right away, Professor Thorn*,' came the same robotic voice the children had heard before.

Behind the professor's back, Olive and Frankie shared a nervous glance. If Professor Thorn turned out to be Shadow, they were willingly entering the lion's den. But it was too late to turn back now. The glass lift began its rapid descent.

Several seconds passed before the lift came to a

gentle stop. 'Here we are, here we are!' Professor Thorn ushered them through the open doors, into a bright corridor. Olive and Frankie blinked. The walls and ceiling were made of a translucent white glass that shone blindingly. It couldn't have felt more different to the entrance above with its timber walls and forest views. 'Above ground, the laboratory would attract too much attention,' explained the professor, sensing their surprise, 'so I keep it hidden away down here.'

Hearing this, Olive couldn't help but wonder why exactly Professor Thorn was so eager to avoid attention. *What's he trying to hide?* she asked herself. *And could it have something to do with Mission Shadow?*

But there was no time to ask Professor Thorn any questions as he set off speedily down the corridor.

The children chased after him, trying not to slip on the smooth floor. On either side, visible through panes of clear glass, were vast rooms filled with glowing computer screens and what looked like giant microscopes. It made the science lab at Olive's school seem positively prehistoric in comparison. The constant hum of machines and the lack of windows to the outside world made Olive feel a bit like she was in a submarine. She half-expected to see a school of tropical fish glide by. What she actually saw was even more astonishing.

There were no people in these labs. Instead, a network of glossy robots worked away, their movements smooth and precise. Stopping at one of the windows for a better look, Olive saw a line of white headband-like objects slowly passing along a conveyor belt that snaked around the room. *Memorisers*. The robots that stood along the belt all seemed to have a different task to complete: adding a part, scanning the device, performing some kind of analysis, packing each one carefully in a box. Frankie pressed his palms to the glass as he peered through, mouth open.

Seeing the looks on the children's faces, Professor Thorn grinned. 'It's pretty amazing, isn't it,' he said proudly. 'Thirteen years ago, most people thought my ambition of capturing memories was impossible. When I tried to convince investors to fund my research, they simply laughed at me. But the challenge of making the impossible happen was exactly what drew me to the idea. Over time, I proved them all wrong. And here,' he said with a flourish as they reached the end of the corridor, 'is the beating heart of the operation.'

Olive and Frankie's jaws dropped. The corridor

had opened out into a vast, cavernous space which, in Olive's opinion, stretched the very definition of the word 'room'. There was no doubt they were now in the main chamber of the laboratory. It was shaped like a huge snail shell, with a walkway that spiralled from the outer edges of the room upwards and inwards towards the ceiling. The closest comparison Olive could draw was to standing in the middle of a helter-skelter ride. Running her eyes up and along the spiral walkway, she tried to guess how many rooms there were leading off it. Doing so was like estimating the quantity of sweets in a jar: both exceptionally difficult and woefully inaccurate.

Most exciting of all, however, was what they saw next. Not far from where they stood was an enormous holographic brain. About the size of a small car, it glowed with blue light and spun slowly. Professor Thorn stopped in front of it. 'The work we conduct here at Forget Me Not is at the cutting edge of research into the mysteries of memory,' he said. 'Did you know, the brain is made up of around one hundred billion neurons, give or take? Right now, the neurons in your brains are firing like the world's most unbelievable firework show. Put your hand up to the light, Olive, and I'll show you.'

Olive and Frankie shared a look. 'Go on, it won't hurt you,' insisted Professor Thorn. Curiosity getting the better of her, Olive reached her palm towards the holographic brain as she'd been told. Sure enough, as soon as she made contact, it was instantly illuminated with countless little stars of light.

'Impressive neural activity,' said Professor Thorn, as Olive took her hand away and Frankie had a go. 'I used holographic technology to help us map the neural networks underlying memory. Once I'd figured out how to map memories, I then had to work out how to copy them on to the device you both know as a Memoriser. These days, that machine can both extract and record memories. And even play them back, too, with the user's own brain becoming a kind of projector.'

'Does it hurt . . . extracting the memories?' asked Olive, thinking of her grandmother.

'You feel a gentle current on your temples,' he replied, 'but that's all. I can show you if you'd like. We can project one of your own memories in holographic form, using that machine over there. It won't be as good as using a Memoriser – nothing can beat your brain when it comes to experiencing memories – but it's good enough.'

The machine he was pointing to was shaped like an upside-down bowl, held aloft by a thin white pole. 'Don't worry, I won't snoop around inside your brain,' Professor Thorn said, laughing. 'You just need to stand underneath it.'

Before Olive could stop him, Frankie stepped forward. He stood so he was directly underneath the bowl and it immediately started lowering towards his head, stopping only when it covered the top half of Frankie's face. 'Think of what you had for breakfast this morning,' instructed Professor Thorn. 'See it in your mind's eye as strongly as you can.'

Frankie closed his eyes in concentration. A second later, beams of light shot up from a rectangular glass-topped table beside the machine. The lights quickly settled into place, taking the form and colours of Frankie's favourite cereal bowl filled with cornflakes, hovering about a metre above the table.

'Wow,' breathed Frankie. 'It tickles.'

'Your turn now, Olive,' said Professor Thorn. Frankie stepped away from the machine and the holographic cereal bowl disappeared.

'No, thank you,' she said regretfully. She worried that if Professor Thorn had access to her memories like that, he might discover something she didn't want him to know, such as his being a suspect in their search for Shadow.

'Suit yourself,' said Professor Thorn, sounding a little put out. 'If we continue up the walkway I can show you the labs where we study long and short-term memory. Our research to enhance memory storage and learning is taking place a little further along. I'm working on a device that would make revising for exams a doddle. This way . . .'

Olive hesitated. There were a million questions she wanted to ask about Professor Thorn's research. She wanted to explore every corner of Forget Me Not. But she couldn't forget their mission. 'Professor Thorn,' she began, holding her brother back, 'before we see anything else, can I ask you some questions about our grandmother?'

Professor Thorn stopped in his tracks, frowning. 'You can, but I didn't really know her very well,' he said carefully. 'We worked together only once, for a short time before I . . . err . . . parted ways with my previous employer.'

Now that they were on the right subject, Olive didn't want to lose Professor Thorn's attention. So, she pushed a little further. 'You worked together while you were still a spy, you mean?'

Professor Thorn's mouth opened with surprise. 'How did you . . . ?' he began, before stopping himself. 'Ah, of course. You probably know that from watching your grandmother's memories, don't you?' Olive nodded, relieved that Professor Thorn had answered his own question. He continued, 'Like I said, I left that line of work to start my own research thirteen years ago now. Before you were born, probably.' He smiled, but the smile didn't reach his eyes. She noted that his jovial tone had stiffened. He glanced down at his watch, as if he was regretting his offer of a tour. 'Now we should be getting on . . .'

Despite his shyness around strangers, Frankie couldn't hide his intrigue. 'Why would you stop being a spy?' he asked, scrunching his nose. He clearly couldn't understand why anyone would willingly give up such an exciting career, even if it were to set up somewhere like Forget Me Not.

Professor Thorn looked taken aback. 'I don't believe that's your business!' he snapped. Frankie took a step back in shock and Professor Thorn seemed to regret his tone. 'I mean, you know how it is . . . I found my calling elsewhere.' He coughed awkwardly. 'I don't really like to discuss it, to be honest. It's been thirteen years since I left espionage. I have

nothing to do with it any more. Absolutely nothing.'
He avoided their eyes, and Olive and Frankie shared
a sideways glance.

By the standards Olive had set out, Professor Thorn
hadn't the *means* nor the *motive* nor the *opportunity*
to be Shadow. He had been away when the Memoriser
was stolen, he hadn't known their grandmother well,
and he claimed not to have had anything to do with
espionage for over a decade. He couldn't have been
Shadow . . . *if* he was speaking the truth. Because
there was no doubt about it – since they'd brought up
his career as a spy, Professor Thorn's mood had
changed dramatically. He'd become cagey and
nervous. Even now, his whole body was tightly
clenched and he was checking his watch anxiously.

Sensing she'd reached a dead end, Olive decided it
was time to try a new approach. It was an approach
she used on her teachers at school whenever she forgot
her homework (which was often) or was late for
registration (which was daily). The approach combined
flattery with an appeal for sympathy. Especially when
used with a lot of sighing and staring down at her
shoes, it had a remarkably high success rate. And
there was something about the professor that told her
it *might* just work on him.

'We're sorry for being so nosy.' Olive stared at the ground humbly. 'I guess we're just curious.'

'No need to apologise,' Professor Thorn mumbled in reply, shoulders slackening. 'As I said before, curiosity is a wonderful thing. Most of the time, anyway.'

'The thing is,' Olive proceeded, 'there's something my brother and I need to tell you. We're not really here for a tour . . . though we feel very lucky to get to see somewhere so incredible . . . so pioneering . . . and to meet a genius such as yourself.' Olive paused, wondering if she was overdoing it, but judging by the more relaxed expression that was now on Professor Thorn's face, she was getting it exactly right. 'There's also something terrible we have to tell you about. Yesterday, not long after it arrived, the Memoriser was stolen.'

'Stolen . . . *stolen?*' he repeated in what seemed like a tone of genuine shock. 'Who would do such a thing?'

'That's exactly what we're trying to find out, Professor Thorn,' Olive replied. 'And we thought that somebody with your brilliant mind might be able to help us.'

At this, Professor Thorn softened again. 'Well, yes . . . I certainly will help, if I can.'

'To start with,' Olive went on, in the same conciliatory tone, 'did anybody else know about Grandma recording her memories, and the Memoriser coming to me?'

'No . . . no of course not . . .' said Professor Thorn, in a deeply offended tone. 'I'm very strict about confidentiality. Only your grandmother and I knew. Oh, and her lawyer, of course.'

'Ms Lowry!' said Frankie. He gave his sister a meaningful look which she knew meant *I told you so*. Olive sighed with frustration. Maybe visiting Forget Me Not *had* been a dead end after all. Maybe Ms Lowry and Howard Sweet *were* to blame for stealing the Memoriser, as Agent Nest had said, and this trip was a waste of time.

'The thing is, Professor Thorn,' Olive began again, not wanting to give up yet, 'it was such an honour to receive the Memoriser. After all, it's not every day you get to encounter such ground-breaking technology. But we barely got to watch any of our grandmother's memories. All we wanted was to get to know her. We know nothing about her life, you see. And without watching her memories, we never will.'

Olive dropped her eyes to the floor again, giving the most miserable look she could manage. After an elbow to the rib from his sister, Frankie caught on and adopted a gloomier expression.

Professor Thorn had the panicked look of somebody who was unprepared for the tricks of children. 'Oh, don't get upset . . . please. We'll work something out.'

'I can't imagine how,' said Olive downheartedly. 'Unless you had copies of the memories . . . ?'

'Of course we do,' Professor Thorn replied sniffily. 'We keep back-up copies of everything.'

'Really?' exclaimed Olive. 'Oh, I knew you would. How wonderful! Can we take a copy with us, please?'

Professor Thorn looked anxious again.

'Or perhaps we could watch them while we're here?' suggested Frankie.

'I suppose . . .' said Professor Thorn uncertainly. His face was scrunched into a frown, as if he was thinking something through. 'I mean, I don't see why not. They were intended for you, after all . . .'

'Thank you, oh thank you!' Olive enthused, as if the deal were done. 'We knew you could help, didn't we, Frankie?'

'Yep!' Frankie nodded enthusiastically.

'Well, OK then.' Professor Thorn nodded to himself decisively. 'I wouldn't usually do this.' He set off towards the walkway. 'But if you both wait down here, I'll retrieve the memories from the archive and get them ready for you to watch. In the meantime, please *don't* wander about. I won't be long.'

# CHAPTER ELEVEN

# Back into the Memories

As soon as Professor Thorn was out of sight, Olive grinned triumphantly at her brother. 'We did it,' she whispered. 'Now we can finally see all the memories that Grandma wanted us to!'

'*And* we've ruled Professor Thorn out as a suspect.' Frankie beamed. 'He wouldn't be rushing to show us the memories if he was Shadow, would he?'

'I guess not,' said Olive. It would have been very strange indeed for Professor Thorn to agree to show them the memories if he'd stolen them just the day before. At the same time, there was something about Professor Thorn's behaviour that was bugging her. She just couldn't quite put her finger on what it was.

Swivelling on his heel, Frankie took in their surroundings. The look in his eye was of a child in a sweet shop with an unlimited credit card in his pocket. 'What a place,' he said breathily. 'It's *weird* to think that Grandma Sylvie came here.'

While her brother was marvelling at the laboratory, Olive ran her eyes over the many rooms that led off from its main chamber. She noticed one of the doors on the ground floor not far from where they were waiting was open, through which she could see what looked like an office. Turning her head to check that the coast was clear, she motioned to her brother.

'Frankie,' she hissed, 'come on. Let's see what's in here. Quickly, before Professor Thorn comes back.'

'But we were told not to wander. What if he comes back and finds us sneaking around?'

Before he could stop her Olive had slipped off in the direction of the office.

'You still think Thorn could be Shadow?' asked Frankie, catching up to her. 'But he doesn't have the means, motive *or* opportunity.'

'I know, I know . . . it's just a feeling I have. He acted so strangely when we questioned him. Like he's hiding something.'

With a last look to make sure the professor wasn't coming back, Olive slipped through the open glass door. The room inside was sparsely decorated and ultra-modern. Hanging on the walls were framed photographs showing Professor Thorn posing with people in fancy dresses and sharply cut suits – rock stars, presidents, even royalty.

Frankie's face was filled with awe. 'Do you think all these famous people have used Memorisers to record their memories?'

Olive shrugged. 'Possibly. Ms Lowry did say the technology is very exclusive.' Her attention drifted to a computer on Professor Thorn's desk. Checking first that the coast was clear, she rushed over to it.

'There could be something on this!' Olive tapped at the screen and it came to life. Her hope flared for a moment, then soured to disappointment. 'Oh. It needs a password. Of course it does.'

'Hmmm,' said Frankie, looking thoughtful. 'There might be some clues about his password in his dossier. People use things that are personal to them, don't they?'

'It's worth a try!' Olive retrieved Professor Thorn's folder from her brother's backpack, opened it up and scanned the information. First, she tried typing in the street in Edinburgh where Professor Thorn lived as a child, then the names of both his parents. Then she tried his birthday. None of them worked.

Olive looked back to Frankie, who was still studying the folder. 'Try "Jekyll and Hyde" – the name of Professor Thorn's huskies. People *always* use their pets as passwords . . . if they're allowed pets,' he finished sadly.

Olive wasn't hopeful. She didn't think a great scientist like Professor Thorn would use something as obvious as the names of his pets as a password. But sure enough, when Olive typed out JEKYLLANDHYDE, the login page vanished. 'We're in!' she cried. 'Good thinking, Frankie.'

Her brother beamed. With a few taps, Olive had opened Professor Thorn's folders. Olive ran her eyes over some of the open documents. She flicked quickly through boring spreadsheets and scientific reports that made her eyes go blurry. Olive was about to start searching for Professor Thorn's emails instead when something caught her attention. It was a document with lots of confusing words and figures. At the top it had the heading:

FINANCIAL REPORT

Olive scanned through rows and rows of numbers. It seemed to be a bank statement of some kind, recording payments in and out of Forget Me Not's business account. 'Wow . . . that's a lot of zeros,'

Olive said, stopping at a particularly large deposit. 'And look, not long after, here's another for the same amount. Frankie, maybe these are payments for selling secrets!' Olive said excitedly, getting ahead of herself as usual, quickly looking through the rest of the rows. 'And there are more! All the big payments have come from somebody called . . . ANN. But I've no idea who that is. Ann who?'

Frankie leaned over her shoulder. 'Take a photo of it with your phone,' he suggested. 'Maybe we can work it out later.'

Olive had just enough time to take a quick shot of the screen before hearing footsteps. She quickly turned off the computer screen and got to her feet. Then, as fast as they could, the children darted away from the desk towards the door.

'Excuse me,' came a voice from the doorway barely a second later. The children stared back, trying their best not to look guilty. 'What are you doing in here?'

'The door was open,' Frankie said quickly, 'and I saw these *amazing* photos on the wall and just wanted to look more closely. How do you know all these cool people?' he asked, sounding impressed. 'You must be pretty famous!'

At this, Professor Thorn smiled graciously. Olive

smiled too and reminded herself to congratulate Frankie later. 'It's certainly true that many important, influential people – like Sylvie Jones herself – have chosen to use our memory technology in recent years.' A faraway look came over his face. 'And many more will be using it very soon . . .'

Olive turned to him. 'Why's that?'

Professor Thorn's smile disappeared. 'You really *are* curious, aren't you?' he said, giving her a piercing look. 'Every bit as inquisitive as Sylvie Jones was.' Then Professor Thorn turned sharply, ushering them out of his office. 'Hurry along, please. Your grandmother's memories are ready for you to watch.'

\*

It was decided that Olive would watch the memories. Her experience of using a Memoriser the day before meant she was already prepared for – although still rather nervous about – the strange sensation of stepping back into her grandmother's memories. Frankie was clearly disappointed about missing out for a second time, but Olive assured him that when they finally managed to recover the Memoriser, he would have the very first go.

Professor Thorn led Olive through the main chamber of the laboratory and into a room not far up the walkway. Entering it, they found that the room was empty except for a control panel at the side and a white leather chair that looked like the kind from a dentist surgery. Encouraged by Professor Thorn, Olive climbed into it, then reclined until she was staring up at the ceiling. At the top of the chair was a helmet-type device, which the professor lowered over her head. He'd already explained that rather than transferring the memories to a Memoriser, which would take some time, they would come straight from the archive. Somehow this made the process seem scarier. Lying in the chair, Olive started to feel nervous, as if Professor Thorn really *was* a dentist and was about to perform a tooth extraction.

'Ready to begin?' he asked, staring down at her.

'Ready.' Olive closed her eyes. She took a deep breath and tried to clear her mind, as she had done the day before. Like the last time, at first nothing happened. Olive spent a minute or two simply staring at the back of her eyelids.

Then, from the darkness, came a vivid swirl of colour, greys and blues and reds and greens. It felt like a daydream was drifting into her head in the same way a cloud moves across the sky. And at the same time, it was as if Olive herself were floating away, lifting out of the chair, out of her body even, and being transported somewhere far away, somewhere that seemed just as real to her as the laboratory had moments before.

A moment later, all trace of Forget Me Not was gone. Olive was in a school science lab, in a headmaster's office. These memories she had seen before. She watched them impatiently. And then . . . she was somewhere new. She was standing outside in bright sunlight. A gentle breeze carried the sweet smell of recently cut grass. Looking around, Olive realised that, to her surprise, she was walking down her own street, only a few houses down from her home. As before, she was watching the memory through her grandmother's eyes. But Olive wasn't sure *when* exactly the memory was taking place. She knew it must have been a long time after the other memories she'd seen, because her grandmother had only moved to live in the bungalow a few years before Olive was born. Despite this, it was reassuring to be back near her home. It was a few moments, however, before Olive looked down and realised, with a gasp, exactly what her grandmother was doing.

She was pushing a pram.

Peering into the pram, Olive had a second, even greater, shock: the little round face staring back at her was, in fact, her own. Her mother had shown Olive enough embarrassing baby photos over the years for Olive to be quite sure. But Olive couldn't *remember* ever going for a stroll with her grandmother.

*Why has nobody told me about this?* she wondered. *Why didn't we walk together when I was old enough to remember?*

Olive was still pondering these questions as she found herself walking through Grandma Sylvie's wooden gate, which wasn't as creaky then as it was now. At the porch, she watched Grandma Sylvie's hands rifle through her bag as if searching for keys. But before she could find them, the bungalow's front door burst open and a person flew through it at speed, knocking the pram with force. Olive watched her grandmother's hands grasp for the pram, only just managing to keep it from turning over. By the time she'd looked up again, the intruder had jumped over the gate and was sprinting down the road.

With the intruder gone, Olive found herself pushing the pram hastily inside the bungalow. The place had been ransacked; picture frames were broken, vases smashed, sofa cushions strewn on the floor. Watching the memory unfold through Grandma Sylvie's eyes, Olive took in the chaotic scene. Somebody had clearly been looking for something. Somebody like Shadow.

Baby-Olive's wails faded away as the memory darkened. Then gradually, another memory appeared. This time, Olive was walking briskly through a park. It was a park she didn't recognise, with a grand stone fountain and the dusty brown grass of peak summer. Around her, Olive could hear people speaking in French and felt a thrill. She'd always wanted to visit France – though of course she'd never dreamed she would do so inside a memory.

Olive was still admiring the scenery when her perspective shifted. Her grandmother must have glanced over her shoulder. Now Olive saw why: somebody was following her. A man with his head dipped and hands in his pockets. He was wearing a flat cap pulled low over his eyes. Olive, watching the scene as if she were Grandma Sylvie, suddenly turned to cross a bridge over a pond. Once across it, she took an immediate right turn, ducking through a gap in a hedge. As the man reached the hedge, Olive-as-Grandma-Sylvie sprang out from behind it, flipping him in an almost complete circle and bringing him down on to the ground. He lay there, startled, looking up his attacker.

'Who sent you to follow me?' Olive heard her grandmother bark, though it felt as if the words had come from her own mouth.

'I don't know what you're talking about,' the man snarled in a French accent. He had a tense, angular jaw and a dimpled chin covered in golden stubble.

'Don't insult me,' Grandma Sylvie shot back. 'You've been following me since the Champs-Élysées. Who do you work for? Tell me!'

'Who do I work for?' The man laughed menacingly, turning Olive's heart to ice. 'Somebody who is always lurking behind you, watching everything you do. Somebody who seems to be just like you but look a little closer and you'll find they are very, *very* different. Somebody who is impossible to catch. Somebody like . . . a shadow.'

Olive sensed her grandmother step backwards. This was all the opportunity the man needed. With a sudden lurch he was back on his feet. Before Olive's grandmother could move, he'd sprinted back on to the path and towards a group of strolling pedestrians. The man slowed to a casual walk as he joined them, straightened his flat cap and, within a matter of seconds, had disappeared into the crowd.

Olive's heart beat wildly. Before she'd had time to recover, everything was fading and colours were swirling as another memory came into focus. This time Olive was standing in a busy restaurant. There was the sound of dinner conversation and the clink of cutlery against plates. At a bar in the back of the restaurant smartly dressed servers shook cocktail shakers behind their shoulders and squeezed fresh limes over ice. A bustling crowd of stylishly dressed people were gathered there, enjoying drinks while they waited for their tables. Olive was standing behind a pillar near the end of the bar. She was half hidden from view, so that anyone at the bar would be unlikely to notice she was there.

For a moment, Olive wasn't sure what exactly Grandma Sylvie was staring at. Then she heard it – somebody had said her grandmother's name. The speaker was only a few metres away, standing with his back to Olive and holding a phone to his ear, speaking in a French accent.

'Yes, it was stolen from Sylvie Jones. Came courtesy of my little friend in the British Intelligence Service . . . Exactly, the one known as Shadow. It has a list of the informants, as we wanted.' The man looked up cautiously. 'We made the exchange over a drink. You know the place. Shadow didn't stay long in case we were followed. I shouldn't either. Goodbye.'

Olive watched the man hang up the phone and slip it into his jacket pocket. He turned to leave the bar area, weaving through the bustling crowd. Olive got a glimpse of his face and realised with a gasp that he was the same man from the last memory, the one with the flat cap and blonde stubble. In a matter of seconds, she'd lost sight of him. As soon as he was gone, Olive-as-Grandma-Sylvie wove through the crowd towards the spot at the bar where the man had been standing. There she saw two drinks, both half empty and diluted by melting ice, beside a napkin folded into the shape of a swan.

But before Olive could search the scene for clues, the memory started to fade. She tried to fight it. She needed to see more. She wanted to follow the blonde man. But that wasn't how it worked. This was a memory, and Olive was only an observer.

The memory darkened to black again and this time it remained dark. Shortly afterwards Olive had the feeling of returning to herself. First, she became aware of her own breathing, of the way her ribcage bobbed up and down. Next, she became aware of a harsh wailing sound like a siren or an alarm. After a short while, it occurred to Olive to open her eyes. She winced at the bright lights of the laboratory.

There was the blurry shape of her brother's head above her. He was watching Olive nervously as if waiting for her to wake up from an operation and saying her name repeatedly.

'Olive! OLIVE! Are you OK?' Frankie asked urgently, having to yell over the noise of the alarm.

It took a moment for Olive to sit up. The memories had been so absorbing, had seemed so real, that switching back to reality was disorienting. She struggled to process everything that she'd just witnessed. There was the break-in at her grandmother's bungalow, the encounter in the park in Paris, and the conversation she'd overheard in the restaurant. Olive instantly wanted to re-watch the memories to look for more clues. They'd ended so quickly.

'Why did it stop?' she asked, still groggy. 'I thought there'd be more . . .' Gradually her ears tuned into the horribly loud noise she'd heard as the memories had faded. It was an alarm ringing out loudly across the laboratory.

'Olive, you have to wake up properly . . . something's going on,' said Frankie.

Blue lights on the walls were flashing urgently. Looking over at Professor Thorn, she saw that he looked aghast.

'What . . . what's happening?' shouted Olive over the noise. Her face showed a look of bewilderment.

'I don't know,' said Frankie, anxiously glancing at Professor Thorn, who was tapping away on the control panel at the side of the room with a look of panic.

A robotic voice, the same one they'd heard on arrival, boomed out of an unseen speaker. *'Professor Thorn, an intruder has accessed the memory archive. Please go straight to the archive to assess the damage. Security will pursue the intruder.'*

Olive turned to Frankie. They mouthed the word in unison. 'Shadow!'

# CHAPTER TWELVE

## The Chase

'You two, wait here,' Professor Thorn told the children sternly. 'I need to find out what's going on.' He gave them a harried look, before hastening out the room and up the walkway towards the archive.

'Do you really think it's Shadow, Olive?' asked Frankie once they were alone again.

Olive nodded. 'Maybe they're trying to wipe the original memories too, cover·their tracks? We *have* to stop them getting away. Come on, let's go, before Professor Thorn comes back!'

The children raced across the laboratory floor and back down the long white corridor. They passed no one as they rushed to the lift, travelled upwards to the ground floor and then sprinted across the lobby, passing the crystal forget-me-not sculpture.

Emerging outside, they saw a lone figure hurrying down the path away from the building. Olive felt a sharp pang of shock. Even from a distance, she recognised him at once. Like in the photograph in his dossier, he had a head of neatly combed greyish hair. He was wearing a brown leather bomber jacket with a white fleece collar. For a man in his early eighties, he moved with remarkable speed and agility.

'It's Howard Sweet!' said Frankie in a breathy whisper. 'Agent Nest was right . . . Howard is Shadow.'

Olive's heartbeat was racing wildly. 'Yes, and this time we've caught him red-handed.' But then Olive saw what was waiting for Howard Sweet at the end of the path. It was a gold car, parked next to their own. *No!* she cried inwardly. *He can't get away again.*

'Come on!' she urged her brother, tugging at his arm. 'Hurry!'

The children sprinted as fast as they could, but it was no good. Howard Sweet was in his car before they were even halfway down the path. The door swooped shut behind him and less than a second later, sending a spray of earth from the turning wheels, Howard Sweet zoomed away, racing down the drive with a dazzling flash of gold.

The next moment three security guards appeared

through the automatic doors. Olive and Frankie darted around the side of the cabin to avoid being seen.

'What do we do now?' whispered Frankie desperately, as they peeked out to watch the guards.

'We need to follow him.' Olive's heart was still thumping against her ribcage. She'd heard herself say the words without taking a moment to think it over.

Her brother's eyes grew wide. 'We can't start a car chase, Olive!' he said. 'You're getting carried away. This isn't one of those action movies you like to watch. It's too dangerous. We should tell Professor Thorn who we saw escaping.'

'No sign of the intruder here,' came the voice of one of the guards, looking out to the end of the drive, not realising how close they'd come to catching the culprit. 'We'll return to secure the other entrances.'

'We don't know for sure that we can trust Thorn,' Olive insisted. 'Besides, the car will do all the work for us. But we have to go right now if we're going to catch up.' With the guards gone, Olive ran from their hiding place and towards their car, hoping Frankie would follow.

Frankie gave a frustrated sigh, then chased after his sister. The car doors shot upwards as they approached, and the children climbed quickly inside. 'Hello . . . We need to follow that gold car. The one that just left. It's important we don't lose it. Can you do that? Please?'

Instantly, the car doors slid shut. Seemingly from nowhere, two seat belts swooped over the children's shoulders, pressing them so firmly back against the velvet seats that they barely had room to breathe.

'*Car-chase mode initiated*,' came the voice of the car. Olive felt a little thrill as the engine came to life and, without further warning, the car lurched forward and off down the drive, just as the gold car had done moments before. The chase had begun.

Trees blurred as the car rocketed along the road.

'There he is!' shouted Olive, catching a glimpse of gold through the front windscreen. The car carrying Howard Sweet was travelling fast, but it was no match for their own.

'What exactly do you plan to do when we reach him?' shouted Frankie frantically as they pulled closer, giving voice to the same thought that had just occurred to Olive.

Truth be told, Olive didn't know what she was going to do. A rush of adrenaline had sent her running to the car. Adrenaline had told her that it would be a good idea to start a car chase, like she'd seen in the movies. But adrenaline hadn't told her what to do next. And now – as the adrenaline was starting to wear off – Olive tried frantically to come up with a plan.

'*Approaching target*,' announced the car, as if it could read her mind. '*Awaiting next instruction.*'

'I'm thinking!' she snapped.

Olive tried to remember how car chases normally ended in films. Sometimes, it occurred to her, they ended with explosions, and she certainly didn't want that. Other times the car being chased got away, and she didn't want that either. One thing was for sure, Olive couldn't remember anybody pulling over willingly in a car chase and giving themselves up.

They also couldn't keep following Howard Sweet for ever. He would notice them soon enough – if he hadn't already. And once he spotted them, there was no way that he'd lead them straight to the Memoriser. If he really was Shadow, he'd have more tricks up his sleeve than that. The children needed the element of surprise.

'The gadgets!' Olive said excitedly. 'Give me your backpack, Frankie . . .'

Buried in her brother's backpack, Olive had remembered, were the spy devices they'd taken from their grandmother's basement, including a tracker pistol, which could be used to launch a tracking dart at Howard Sweet's car. Olive had been cross at herself for not memorising the address written in Ms Lowry's diary before giving it to Agent Nest. Now they could find out where Howard lived and hopefully where he was keeping the Memoriser. It wouldn't matter then if they lost him – in fact, they could let him get away. They'd be able to find him later.

'What do you want from it?' asked her brother as he wriggled it off his back and handed it over.

'I have a plan,' she told Frankie. 'I need the tracker pistol.'

'The tracker pistol?' he replied. 'What are you . . . oh! You're going to shoot the tracker at his car so we can track him from a distance! That's clever!'

'*I* thought so,' Olive said, with a hint of a smile. She unzipped her brother's backpack and started rooting through the gadgets. 'Where is it? It must be in here somewhere.' She pulled out her brother's uneaten lunch (which he gladly took, selecting a sandwich to nibble on) and an exercise book that had been squashed beneath it. 'Got it!' said Olive, extracting the tracker pistol triumphantly. She looked at it for a moment, trying to figure out how it worked, then addressed the robotic driver.

'Keep following that gold car,' she said. 'But hold

back a little, so he can't see what we're up to. And please can you release my seatbelt just a little?'

The car did as she'd instructed. Their speed reduced and Olive and Frankie found they were no longer pressed to the back of their seats. They turned on to a roundabout, following Howard Sweet's car as it took the second exit. At that point, Olive was able to unbuckle the heavy seat belt.

'Car, please can you open the roof window?'

A second later, the window above Olive's head slowly opened. Cool wind whipped through the vehicle bringing with it the smells of the countryside.

Olive closed the table of snacks and climbed up on to it. Cautiously, she poked the top of her head through the gap. From below, her brother handed her the tracker pistol. She raised the barrel out of the window. Closing one eye, Olive peered through the eye piece with the other and aimed at the gold bumper ahead.

With a deep breath, she steadied herself. Then she pulled the trigger. The tracker pistol fired, jolting Olive backwards. With an audible *woosh*, the tracker dart flew from the gun.

Olive ducked back down into the car. Her breathing was fast, her head spinning. She fought the urge to pop up again and take a peek. She couldn't risk

Howard seeing her. Climbing down off the table and back into her seat, Olive glanced at her brother, who was looking up at her in awe.

'Did it hit?' Frankie asked.

Olive rummaged through Frankie's backpack again, this time retrieving a square device that looked like a small tablet. When she turned it on, it synced to the tracker pistol, and a moment later *two* little red dots appeared on a map, one of them racing ahead of the other. 'YES! We're officially tracking Howard Sweet's car!' Frankie gave Olive an enthusiastic high five. Then, overcome with light-headedness, she sat backwards on the velvet seat.

'*Where to now, Miss Jones?*' asked the car politely.

'Back to the bungalow, please,' replied Olive, as her head began to steady. 'Quick as you can. There's something I want to check out.'

*

As they drove back to their grandmother's basement, Olive filled Frankie in about what she'd seen in the memories. When they arrived back at the bungalow, Frankie took the chance to rest in an armchair while they waited for the tracker to tell them Howard's location. Olive, however, couldn't sit still. The shifty way Professor Thorn had behaved was bothering her. It had felt like he was hiding something – something to do with his reasons for leaving espionage thirteen years before. According to the dossiers, Professor Thorn's final mission was called Operation Beehive. Perhaps something had happened during that operation which caused him to change career? And perhaps that was somehow connected to Mission Shadow? It might have been nothing, but since they had some time to kill, Olive thought it wouldn't hurt to check it out.

Setting down the tracker, she went over to her grandmother's cabinets and started rifling through the files inside, looking for one marked *Operation Beehive*. Flicking past folders marked enticingly with *Operation Bearclaw* and *Operation Blackbird*, she soon found the right one, a thick folder filled with photographs and a detailed report. Scanning through it, she quickly found Professor Thorn's name. According to the report, he'd overseen all the gadgets used for the operation. Then, flinching with surprise, she spotted another name she recognised.

'Violet Nest,' she said wonderingly.

Frankie's head popped round the armchair. 'What's

going on?' he asked.

'It's just a weird coincidence in one of these files,' said Olive slowly. 'I was investigating Operation Beehive because the dossier says it was Professor Thorn's last mission. But it turns out it was also Violet Nest's last mission. Agent Nest's mother, remember? The one who was friends with Grandma. It says she went to meet a source who she thought had valuable information . . . only it turned out to be a trap. She was badly injured and eventually died. Poor Violet Nest.'

'Poor Natasha Nest, too,' replied Frankie. 'Losing her mother like that.'

'Operation Beehive was thirteen years ago,' Olive continued. 'The same time Shadow started targeting Grandma. They have to be connected.'

Frankie looked uncertain. 'Maybe. But we caught Howard Sweet red-handed stealing memories. You found evidence that Ms Lowry was passing information to people she shouldn't have. We've solved Mission Shadow. What does it matter?'

'I'm just curious, that's all,' replied Olive. 'Professor Thorn acted so oddly when we asked him why he left spying. I wonder if it was because of something that happened during Operation Beehive. Did he have something to do with the death of Violet Nest? I don't know why that would make him target Grandma as Shadow, though . . .'

Frankie frowned, his shoulders slackening. 'I don't know either. But I don't think we should worry too much about it.'

'I suppose you're right,' Olive reluctantly agreed. 'I just don't like unanswered questions. You know they make my imagination go into overdrive.' With a sigh, she put down the folder on Operation Beehive and walked over to the desk to check the tracker. When she saw the flashing light had stopped moving across the map, her heart jumped in her chest.

'Frankie, we've got him!' Olive held up the tracker screen excitedly. 'We know the location of Howard Sweet's hiding place.'

# CHAPTER THIRTEEN

# Howard's Hiding Place

As the car drove away from their grandmother's bungalow, Olive could see Frankie was nervous. They were about to confront a mole, after all – a man who they suspected had spent years tricking their grandmother. If they were correct, Howard Sweet was a seriously dangerous person. And now they were deliberately putting themselves in his path.

Olive did her best to reassure her brother that, if everything went well, they wouldn't have to confront Howard Sweet at all. The car was taking them to the GPS coordinates located by the tracker. Her plan was that they'd sneak in to wherever he was hiding, steal the Memoriser back, and get out of there before anybody noticed they were there. If they got hold of the Memoriser, they could *finally* watch the rest of the memories which Olive was now convinced would hold clues proving Howard Sweet was Shadow. And with that evidence, the children could clear their grandmother's name.

Olive's knee tapped up and down and her brother, humming to himself, rifled through the remaining snacks. He took out a chocolate bar, nibbled at a corner and then returned it, before taking a big bite a few moments later.

'More snacks, Frankie?' asked Olive, managing a smile.

'I eat when I'm nervous, OK?' he said defensively, through a mouthful of chocolate.

After what seemed like an hour at least, the car turned off the main road, and Olive and Frankie found themselves travelling towards a row of red-brick houses at the end of a cul-de-sac. The neighbourhood wasn't at all what either of the children had expected when they'd thought of Howard Sweet's hiding place. They'd imagined a derelict warehouse or somewhere high-tech and top secret. The place they were approaching had windows with flowery curtains and neatly trimmed shrubbery, and a sign that read 'CAREWOOD RESIDENTIAL HOME'.

'A residential home.' Olive frowned. 'This can't

be right.'

Consulting the tracker screen, she saw that the little red dot representing the children's location had nearly merged with the one for Howard Sweet's gold car. And sure enough, as they drove around the side of the building, there it was, parked in one of the spaces by the care home entrance.

With a nervous glance at each other, the children got out of their car. Olive's mouth was very dry. Her stomach felt tight. She could tell Frankie was just as worried. But she pressed on anyway. Throwing her shoulders back, she led the way through the front door. Standing behind a desk was a woman wearing a light blue uniform and holding a clipboard. She was flipping through pages muttering to herself and hadn't noticed the children enter. Olive and Frankie stood uncertainly, waiting for her to look up. She had a name badge that read MANAGER.

'Oh! Hello there,' she said, spotting them at last. 'I didn't hear you come in. How can I help you two?'

Olive tried her best to sound grown up. 'Good . . . umm . . . afternoon. Is Howard Sweet here, please?'

The woman smiled kindly. 'Mr Sweet? Yes, he's one of our newest residents. Only moved in yesterday. Are you here to see him?'

'Yes, we're his . . . grandchildren,' Olive lied.

'How nice for him. He isn't too keen on having visitors . . . but I'm sure he'll make an exception for you two. Right this way.'

Frankie gave Olive a worried look as they followed the woman down the hall. 'Is this really the right place?' he whispered. 'Shouldn't we break away and search for the Memoriser?'

Olive could only shrug. 'That was the plan . . . but then coming somewhere like this definitely wasn't,' she whispered. 'Let's stick with the manager for now. Howard won't hurt us when she's around.' *Or at least I hope he won't*, she thought nervously.

'Your grandfather is in here with some of our other residents,' the manager told them as they entered a bright conservatory. Elderly men and women were sitting on cushioned wicker armchairs. The sunlight streaming through the windows gave the room a sleepy, warm feel. On the far side, sitting at a table playing a game of chess with a befuddled-looking opponent, was the man they knew to be Howard Sweet.

'I've got you now,' he growled, as he placed a piece down triumphantly. 'Try getting out of that one!'

'Excuse me, Mr Sweet,' interrupted the manager

as they approached. 'Awfully sorry \ to interrupt your game.'

'What do you want now?' he grumbled, without turning his head. His tongue was sticking out as he focused on plotting his next move.

'You have visitors, Mr Sweet,' said the woman patiently. 'Two of them, in fact.'

The effect on Howard Sweet was instantaneous. He leapt to his feet so quickly that it made Olive, Frankie and the manager all jump backwards. His eyes were alert, knees slightly bent, arms held out protectively, as if ready to engage in hand-to-hand combat. There was a murmur of surprise from the other residents who were clearly not used to such displays of agility. He frowned suspiciously at Olive, then at Frankie. Then his eyes darted back to the manager.

'I told you no visitors,' he said gruffly. 'Under *any* circumstances.'

'But they're your *grandchildren*, Mr Sweet,' the manager replied, blinking with surprise. 'I thought you might want an . . . exception made . . . for them?'

Olive opened her mouth and then closed it. She was sure Howard Sweet would immediately correct the manager and they would be thrown out. To her surprise, he turned away from her dismissively and focused his eyes on the children. 'Why are you here?' he demanded, eyes flitting between Olive and Frankie. 'Who sent you?'

Olive chose her words carefully. She needed to keep her lie going about being his grandchildren. 'Nobody sent us,' she said gently. 'We just want to see you, *Grandad*. We thought you could tell us some of your stories . . . like the ones about Grandma *Sylvie*,' she added meaningfully.

Howard narrowed his eyes. It was clear he was thinking. A beeping sound came from a gadget on the manager's belt. 'Oh, I'm being called. You three will be OK without me for a minute, won't you?' She looked uncertain.

'Yes, we'll be fine, thank you,' Olive replied. 'Won't we, Grandad?'

In response, Howard Sweet only clenched his jaw. Olive was relieved when the manager tutted and left, apparently taking his silence as agreement. As she walked away, Howard's stiff position softened slightly, his arms dropped and his back straightened, though his eyes didn't leave the siblings for a second.

'Let's walk in the garden,' he said finally. 'If you will excuse me, Gloria.' His chess competitor nodded, looking relieved to have more time to plan her next move.

Howard Sweet opened a set of glass double doors and the children followed him outside to a small but immaculate garden, enclosed by fences on either side and a hedge at the end. Rose bushes with pink blooms were dotted around the perimeter, looking beautiful in the summer afternoon light.

'So,' Howard Sweet began, frowning, 'I take it you're Sylvie's grandchildren? And, as you're both here, I'm guessing you also know what your grandmother did for a living.'

'Yes,' said Frankie. 'We know *everything*.'

At this, Howard gave a hoarse laugh. 'Highly doubtful. But you know enough to have brought you here, which isn't nothing.'

'You're right,' said Olive coolly. 'We don't know everything. For instance, we don't know why *you* decided to betray our grandmother.'

A powerful feeling of anger was bubbling under her skin. This beautiful garden wasn't the kind of place she expected to have such a confrontation, but it would do.

At Olive's words, Howard's eyes widened with shock. Then he recovered himself and his frown returned. 'We'll get into all that. First, tell me how you found me here. Does anybody else know of this location? Are you sure you weren't followed?'

'Nobody else knows. We put a tracker on your car,' Olive replied. 'It led us right to you.'

'Put a tracker on my . . .' Howard Sweet let out a breath. 'You really are Sylvie's grandkids, aren't you?'

'Yes, we are,' replied Olive. Her chin was raised proudly. 'We're the rightful owners of Grandma Sylvie's memories and we're here to get them back. And we're going to clear her name. And most importantly, we're going to stop you from selling any more secrets!'

'Stop *me* . . .' His voice trailed off as he paused by one of the rose bushes. 'You two have got this all figured out, haven't you?' He gently lifted a flower, admired it, and then let it go. 'Tell me. What makes you so sure that *I* betrayed your grandmother?'

Olive was incensed. 'Because about an hour ago we caught you red-handed stealing her memories from Forget Me Not,' she began. '*And* you stole the Memoriser from me yesterday. All because you wanted to stop us from finding out your secret. But we know all about it now. We know *exactly* who you are.'

'And who is that?' Howard Sweet asked calmly.

Olive almost snarled the word. 'Shadow.' Olive waited for him to deny her accusation, daring him to. But she was not prepared for the words that finally came out of his mouth.

'That's *partly* true,' he said, as if it were a matter of fact. 'I did steal the Memoriser.'

Olive and Frankie gawped at one another. 'You admit it!' Olive spluttered. 'You admit that you're Shadow?'

'Not quite.' Howard shook his head. 'You've done well to discover everything you have. You followed the clues well. But you're jumping to the wrong conclusions.' Olive opened her mouth to interrupt, to defend their investigative work and to tell him there was no point in lying. Before she could, Howard raised his palm to silence her. 'I *did* break into your house yesterday afternoon to take the Memoriser, after Ms Lowry informed me of its whereabouts,' he continued. 'And you *did* catch me escaping Forgot Me Not a few hours ago. But I am not – nor have I ever been – the mole known as Shadow. The very suggestion is the deepest insult you could throw at me.'

Olive stared back at Howard, stunned. Howard looked every bit as insulted as he claimed to be, his cheeks drawn in as if he were sucking a lemon.

That moment a realisation hit Olive like a blow to the face. How could she have not seen it before? Not once had she stopped to consider the possibility that the person who stole the Memoriser might *not* actually be Shadow. From the start she'd assumed they had to be the same person. Was that a critical mistake? Could she have got it completely wrong? And was there a chance Howard was telling the truth?

'You *must* be Shadow,' said Frankie. 'Otherwise why would you want to steal the Memoriser? You had motive, means *and* opportunity! Didn't he, Olive?'

'I stole the Memoriser precisely because I am *not* Shadow,' Howard interjected, before Olive could say a word. For the first time, his voice was slightly raised. His eyes shone with emotion as she stared down at Olive and her brother. Olive looked over to the conservatory where a few of the residents were glancing out the windows at them, clearly wondering what Howard and his grandchildren were arguing about. Olive gave them a small nod to indicate that everything was fine, though she would have preferred to tell them to mind their own business.

'I stole the Memoriser to clear your grandmother's name,' continued Howard Sweet in a quieter voice. 'After those awful rumours about her started to circulate, I knew what I had to do. We often didn't see eye to eye, and at times I was a stubborn fool. But after so many years of friendship I couldn't allow her reputation to be destroyed like that. I left the Service immediately so I could devote my time to finding out who was trying to frame her. I tracked down her lawyer, Edith Lowry, to see if she knew anything. When she let slip about the Memoriser, I thought I'd hit the jackpot. I felt certain that Sylvie's memories would prove that she had nothing to do with the terrible actions of the mole.' His eyes fell to the floor. 'Except . . .'

Howard walked forward, hiding his face. Olive waited for him to continue. 'Except what?' she urged impatiently.

'Except that when I watched the memories . . . let's just say that they were not what they should have been.'

Now Olive was really confused. 'What do you mean, "not as they should have been"?'

'I thought the memories would prove her innocence. Instead, the opposite was true. They make it look like Sylvie *was* the mole. But believe me, that's not true. Nobody had more integrity than Sylvie Jones. Her memories had been tampered with.'

Olive had to close her eyes and rub her temple. It was too much to take in at once. 'You're saying,' she began, trying her best to understand, 'that the memories stored on the Memoriser weren't Grandma Sylvie's real memories.' She was thinking of the memories she'd seen in her house yesterday, and of those she'd seen earlier at Forget Me Not.

'Most of the memories were real. Only some of them had been subtly edited, to frame her as Shadow. And, unless you were there yourself, at the moment the memory was made, you wouldn't be able to tell the difference between what really happened and what was fiction. Only your grandmother would have been able to tell for certain.'

'Is that really possible?' asked Frankie. 'To change memories like that?'

Howard Sweet nodded sadly. 'Apparently so.'

'But,' Olive began doubtfully, 'the memories we saw today at Forget Me Not didn't frame Grandma.'

Howard's eyes shone. 'I'm sure that Thorn intended to show you the edited memories. But then I turned up and scuppered his plan. Something I did in the archive must have confused things, so he started showing you the real ones by mistake.'

'I guess that would explain why Professor Thorn

was happy to show us the memories, even if he is Shadow,' said Frankie. 'If he'd edited them to frame Grandma Sylvie, he would have wanted to *make sure* we saw them.'

'But why were you at Forget Me Not today, Howard?' Olive asked suspiciously. 'Why did you want to take even more memories?' Not a second after the question had passed her lips, a realisation struck her. 'Wait . . . was it to get the *real* memories?'

Howard Sweet almost looked impressed. 'Precisely.'

'And did you get them?' asked Frankie.

'Of course.' Howard's lip curled into a smile. 'I might be getting on in age, but I'm still one of the best spies in the business. I was in and out of there while Professor Thorn and his security guards were busy chasing their tails! You two, however, managed to give me a bit more trouble . . .'

'So that's why the memories suddenly cut out,' said Olive, more to herself than anyone else. She'd started pacing on the spot so furiously the grass beneath her feet would soon be worn to dirt. 'If what you're saying is true – and I'm not saying I believe you,' she added quickly, 'that *must* mean that Professor Thorn is Shadow. Only he had the ability to edit the memories before they came to me, using his lab equipment. And only Shadow would *need* to edit the memories to frame someone else. And he could have done it any time at his lab. Means and opportunity!'

'My thoughts exactly,' replied Howard Sweet sombrely.

'But why?' asked Olive slowly. 'I mean . . . why did he *become* Shadow in the first place? What was his motive?'

Howard Sweet looked thoughtful, then his shoulders sank. 'I'm afraid I've no idea what his motive might be. Other than greed.'

'But Grandma Sylvie was sure it was about more than money,' Olive replied. 'She said it had to be personal.'

'Operation Beehive,' said Frankie under his breath.

Olive looked at her brother, taken by surprise.

'Professor Thorn's final mission,' Frankie explained to Howard. 'We found a folder about it. It's called Operation Beehive.'

'Oh yes,' said Howard, hands clasped behind his back. 'I know that mission well. It went awfully wrong. A tragedy . . .'

'Something which happened during that mission must have caused Professor Thorn to quit espionage,' Olive interrupted. 'It has to be connected to Violet

Nest's death. I just know it. He acted suspiciously when we asked him about leaving espionage. Maybe whatever happened led him to become Shadow as well.'

'That would make sense,' said Howard, eyebrows raised. 'A grudge over a failed mission . . . that could explain why he'd want to jeopardise Sylvie's career like Shadow has.'

Frankie looked unsure. 'But Grandma said that Shadow had to be somebody who still worked as a spy. Otherwise, they couldn't have got close enough to steal the kinds of secrets they stole. Professor Thorn hasn't been a spy for thirteen years.' He looked at his shoes, before adding in a whisper, 'Unlike you.'

Olive looked at her brother. 'Frankie's right. Why should we trust you, anyway?'

'The honest answer is you *shouldn't* trust me,' replied Howard Sweet. 'You can't trust anybody in this business. Spies will tell you anything if it gets them closer to what they want. So, I won't ask you to trust me. But I will ask you to follow your instincts. Pay more attention to what people *do* than what they *say*.'

Olive considered this. She remembered a similar conversation from the day before with Agent Nest where she'd asked the same question. *How can I trust you?* Agent Nest had given a very different answer to

Howard Sweet. Agent Nest had given evidence, a reason to trust her. And yet, somehow, Olive found Howard's response more convincing.

'Can you show us the memories – the real ones?' asked Olive finally. 'That's the only way we'll know for sure you're telling the truth.'

Howard Sweet's face fell. 'Unfortunately, it's not that simple. I thought I'd managed to transfer the real memories on to a new Memoriser. But when I got back here and tried to watch them, I found they were scrambled . . . entirely unwatchable. I don't have the technology here to fix them. But I don't need to see the original memories to know the ones I saw were doctored. One memory suggested that your grandmother met a known enemy of the British Intelligence Service at a bar and handed over classified documents. There's no way she would have done that.'

Olive blinked. 'I saw that memory! But Grandma wasn't there to sell secrets. She was hiding behind a pillar on the trail of the real Shadow!' Olive frowned as she thought it all through. 'There has to be something we can do to watch the rest of the original memories,' she said. 'What about at spy headquarters in London? Surely there will be people there who can help to unscramble them?'

That moment, the manager appeared at the glass doors. She was smiling but had a look of worry on her face too. 'Everything all right, you three?'

'Yes, thanks!' sang the children in unison, giving their best smiles. The manager nodded and retreated into the conservatory. As soon as she was gone again, Howard Sweet turned back to Olive, and nodded.

'It's worth a shot,' he said in a fierce whisper. 'And at least it will get me away from this place for a while.'

'Why *are* you here, anyway?' Olive asked.

'It's the one place that nobody would ever expect me to be,' he replied. 'An agent tried to track me down yesterday – thanks to Edith Lowry's carelessness, no doubt – and I only narrowly escaped.' Olive felt a jab of guilt at hearing this, knowing that she was responsible for telling Agent Nest where to find Howard, but decided there was no need to bring this up right now. 'I had to lie low for a while. And this seemed the perfect place. Until you two walked in, that is!' A look of worry flicked across his face. 'How did you two get here, anyway?'

'We took Grandma Sylvie's car,' replied Frankie proudly.

On hearing this, Howard grimaced. 'What's wrong?' asked Olive.

'I wouldn't put it past Shadow to be tracking the car. Somebody might be on their way here as we speak.'

Olive and Frankie shared a worried look. 'You really think so?'

'I'd bet on it,' Howard replied dryly. 'We'll take the train to London instead. The station isn't far.' The children nodded. 'Let's get moving. I'll get my things.'

He paced quickly across the lawn towards the conservatory, a spring in his step. 'Sorry, Gloria, old gal,' he said as he threw open the double doors. 'It looks like our rematch will have to wait. There's still life in this old spy yet!'

# CHAPTER FOURTEEN

# Journey to London

'We have to move fast,' said Howard Sweet as they marched down the road, leaving behind the two abandoned cars, parked conspicuously in front of the sleepy retirement home. 'There's a good chance we're already being followed.'

Howard led the charge, frequently glancing around him for anyone in pursuit. The two children trailed behind, feeling as if they were back in a school P.E. lesson (just one of many lessons Olive and Frankie had missed that day).

When they arrived at the station, Howard bought three tickets to London while Olive checked the screen for their platform. They had seven minutes to wait for the next train.

Olive and Frankie, who was suddenly feeling

famished again, went to a vending machine to buy themselves a snack. It was while her brother was deciding between crisp flavours (the kind of decision he always agonised over) that Olive first noticed the man on the other side of the tracks. Leaning casually against a pillar, he was dressed in blue jeans and a plain T-shirt with a flat cap pulled down low over his eyes. Though the top half of his face was obscured, Olive could make out a dimpled chin with a rash of blonde stubble.

As Olive continued to stare, the man straightened up, catching eyes with Olive for the briefest moment, before quickly looking away. Then he strolled over to a small coffee stand and began talking to the person behind the counter. Forgetting all about her brother and the crisp-flavour dilemma, Olive walked along the platform, tilting her head so she could get a look at the man's face.

Though Howard had warned them that there was a chance they'd be followed, Olive hadn't taken it seriously. And yet there was something about this man that gave her an unsettled feeling. She could have sworn she'd seen him before. But where?

Accepting a cup of coffee over the counter, the man gave the server a brusque 'thanks' in response.

As the sound of his voice floated across the tracks, a realisation hit Olive. The second she heard his French accent she knew exactly why she recognised him – but it wasn't from her own life. It was the man she'd seen in her grandmother's memories, the one who had been following Grandma Sylvie in the Parisian park, the one who she'd overheard on the phone in the restaurant talking about stolen documents. Olive stared wide-eyed as he sipped his coffee and headed calmly in the direction of the stairs. It was only when he reached the first step and began climbing slowly upwards towards the bridge leading over to their platform that the spell was broken. Suddenly aware that she was trembling, she raced back to her brother.

'Frankie,' Olive spluttered, finding her brother clutching a bag of ready-salted crisps with a look of regret on his face, 'there's a man on the other platform. He's *dangerous*. I saw him in one of Grandma's memories. We have to tell Howard right now.'

Frankie turned white and nodded, and they ran back to Howard and found him studying the board. 'Two minutes delayed,' he said with a grumble, as he saw them approaching. 'I'd like to know who's running this operation.'

'Howard, you were right,' said Olive breathlessly.

'We *are* being followed. I saw a man on the platform over there. He's on his way over to our platform. He works for Shadow. I know he does.'

As Olive described the man she'd seen, Howard's eyebrows shot up in recognition. 'That description certainly sounds familiar.' He peered suspiciously along the platform. It was filled with travellers doing crossword puzzles, eating egg and cress sandwiches, or otherwise minding their own business. There was no sign of the man Olive had described. 'He was just there,' she said urgently. 'Really, I promise, Howard.'

Olive was well acquainted with the feeling of not being believed. She knew the exact look of impatience that came across the faces of adults who thought she was lying. It usually came before a lecture about *the little girl who cried wolf* or a warning that children who told fibs grew boils on their tongues. As she'd told plenty of fibs in her life and had not once been eaten by a wolf or developed a mouthful of boils, Olive thought that it was in fact the adults themselves who'd got carried away with their imaginations. But she knew that pointing this out would only result in even more outlandish warnings about what happened to children who answered back. More and more, Olive was learning to hold her tongue (which thankfully remained boil-free) and to keep her imaginings to herself. But that wasn't an option this time. Howard simply *had* to believe her about the man she'd seen, otherwise they'd all be in mortal danger. 'Honestly,' she said, 'I think he's coming right this way.'

But staring up into Howard's steadfast, cool-blue eyes, Olive couldn't see a trace of the doubt she was expecting to see. Instead, he nodded firmly. 'The train will be here in –' he checked the board – 'forty-seven seconds. We won't be able to lose him now. But let's at least put some distance between us.' With a march, he set off down the platform. 'Come on. This way.'

They were reaching the end of the platform with nowhere else to go when they saw him. To Olive's surprise, as he walked along the platform the man didn't show any interest in their presence; in fact, he didn't so much as glance their way. He simply stood there staring down at his phone.

'Has he seen us?' asked Frankie, tapping his foot nervously.

'Without a doubt.' Howard's voice was low. 'Rest assured our friend will be coming with us to London.'

'He's a really dangerous man.' Olive was thinking over the memory she'd seen that morning. 'I could tell by the way he talked to Grandma. She handled him OK, though. Managed to get him flat on the floor with only a few kicks.'

Despite his anxious expression, Howard Sweet let out a laugh. 'That certainly sounds like your grandmother. She could have taken on a raging bull and lived to tell the tale.'

Olive thought again of the portrait of Grandma Sylvie she'd seen at her funeral. Though the photograph was miles away, it felt like her grandmother's eyes were boring straight into her, challenging her, encouraging her. The more she knew about Grandma Sylvie, the more Olive wanted to be just like her. At the same time, the shoes of the legendary Sylvie Jones felt far too enormous to ever be filled.

When at last the train arrived, the three of them stepped forward towards the doors. Olive watched as further down the platform the man did the same thing. The train doors opened and Howard Sweet climbed on board, followed quickly by Frankie. Olive held back. Her eyes were fixed on the man standing halfway down the platform. He hadn't got on the train yet, though the doors in front of him were open. Olive was still watching when his head turned. For a moment, to Olive's horror, he stared directly back at her. His expression was blank, unreadable. Then he stepped on to the train. The doors gave a beeping noise, and Olive clambered on too, just in time, before they closed behind her. A moment later, the train was off, gathering speed as it pulled out of the station. They were on their way to London.

*

Train travel can be a relaxing mode of transport, a time for staring out of windows and getting lost in your own thoughts. This was not that kind of trip. The children spent the entire journey watching the carriage door carefully in case their *friend* from the platform appeared. They sat in the busiest section of the carriage they could find, hoping that he would be put off from approaching them by the number of onlookers.

Olive wouldn't let herself be distracted by anything – not by glimpses of passing countryside through the windows, or by the couple arguing over who was hogging the middle armrest, or by the young boys taking turns to throw grapes into a sleeping woman's handbag. Barely an hour later, the announcement came that they would soon arrive in London. Olive was immediately struck with anxiety about what could happen next. Their follower might have considered it too risky to confront them on the train with so many potential witnesses, but it would be a different story once they stepped off. Olive knew that London was a city where people walked around with blinkers over their eyes, a place full of hidden alleyways and dark corners. It was the perfect place to follow somebody – or to do even worse – without anybody noticing.

The moment the train slowed, Howard rose from his seat. 'Get your tickets ready,' he instructed, moving towards the doors. 'Here's what we do. When we get into the station concourse, we need to find the entrance to the London Underground and head there as quickly as we can. It will be easier to lose our friend down there. It's only seven stops from there to spy headquarters.' He took out his phone and showed them a photograph of a building. 'This is it. The place we need to get to. Understood?' Olive and Frankie nodded. 'However tempted you might be, *don't* look back for him. And don't run. But don't dawdle either. And whatever happens, keep moving.'

Waiting for the train doors to open, Olive felt as if they were at the start of a race. Any moment, the pistol would sound. The doors beeped again to indicate they were unlocked and Olive pressed the button to open them. One after the other, they jumped down on to the platform. As Howard had instructed, they didn't check whether the man was behind them, and they didn't run. With the widest strides they could manage, almost running but not quite, they set off towards the ticket gates. Olive didn't even allow herself to turn towards her brother, who was by her side and managing to keep up well. Arriving at the ticket turnstile, Olive ushered Frankie through the gate first, making sure he got safely through before slotting in her own ticket.

Once through the barriers, they raced across the concourse. Olive knew that her brother would hardly remember their holiday to London five years before and so would be encountering the hugeness of everything as if for the first time. She thought of their mother and how worried she'd be to know that they were in the city without her. Olive reached over and took Frankie's hand, feeling him squeeze her fingers tightly.

With relief, Olive saw a set of escalators with an UNDERGROUND sign just ahead of them. It was only then that she finally gave in to her urge to turn her head. She scanned faces in the crowd, looking for the man's flat cap and dimpled chin. There was nothing . . . nothing . . . then, her stomach turning to ice, Olive's eyes met his. She turned to warn the others, finding herself at the top of the escalator. If Howard hadn't been standing right in front of her, she would have tripped and fallen all the way to the bottom, taking Frankie with her.

'I *said* don't turn around,' Howard hissed through gritted teeth.

Even over the noise of the escalators, Olive could hear her thundering heartbeat. 'He's right behind us, Howard!' she wailed.

Howard gave a low growl. 'Come on then!'

With the energy and pace of a soldier, Howard marched down the steps. Olive and Frankie flew after him, bumping into shoulders and bags as they went. Olive didn't dare look back again. At the bottom, Howard quickly turned right down a long tunnel. Olive was faintly aware of a voice over an intercom warning passengers to walk rather than run while in the station. As if encouraged by this message, Olive moved *even* faster, making impressive pace towards a junction at the end of the tunnel. She was so focused on their destination that she didn't notice that she and

Frankie had overtaken Howard Sweet, who though extremely fit for his age, and a fast runner, was still a man in his eighties.

'Take the next left,' he ordered from behind them, his cheeks reddened.

'We'll wait!' Olive shouted back.

'No!' he roared. 'Keep going! I'll catch up. Go, go!'

Reluctantly, Olive did as she was told. Turning left as they'd been instructed, the children found themselves at the top of a set of steps. Despite Howard's instructions, they waited there for him to appear, then as soon as they had sight of him again, they flew down the steps. Olive could hear the rumble of a train and knew there was one approaching the platform below.

At the bottom of the stairs, a crowd of shuffling commuters blocked the narrow entrance of the platform. 'We're stuck!' Olive shouted. 'There's too many people.'

'Rush hour,' replied Howard, finally catching up. His greyish hair was ruffled and sweat ran down his face. 'We can use that to our advantage. You two are small, push your way through as fast as you can. But don't get the train on this platform. Go down the first passageway, down some more stairs and then take a right turn. Get on the very next train you come to after that. It's seven stops, remember. Get to headquarters and ask for Sir Bobbie Eden. Show him the Memoriser and ask for somebody to unscramble the real memories. Now go! And don't wait for me again, whatever happens!'

'But—' Frankie began, clearly pained at the idea of leaving their new friend behind.

'No buts!' Howard barked, cutting him off. 'GO!'

'Come on, Frankie,' Olive said with a grimace. She hated leaving Howard too, but she could see his mind was made up. On the platform below, people were packed together, shoulder to shoulder, chin to back. They shuffled forwards like cattle. It was hard to spot a gap, but as soon as she saw one, Olive pounced, dragging Frankie behind her.

'Excuse me, please.' Olive pushed through the coats and handbags. Howard Sweet had been right; they were small enough that with a little jostling of elbows they could weave between people. Olive tightened her grip on her brother's hot hand, knowing that if they lost each other here it would be almost impossible to find one another again.

Finally, they reached the passageway with relief. As Howard had told them, there was yet another set of stairs. They took them two at a time, relieved not to be pushing past people any more. At the bottom, they turned right as directed and headed towards the busy platform ahead. They could hear the screech of a train approaching.

'Where's Howard?' shouted Frankie.

'He said he'll catch us up,' replied Olive. 'Keep going!'

When they reached the platform, there was a train sitting waiting with open doors. Olive had a split second to decide what to do. Howard had insisted they get straight on the train. But could they really leave him behind? As well as hating the idea of leaving him, Olive wasn't keen on the idea of them being in London alone either. Though in theory Olive had always found the prospect of no adult supervision exciting, in practice it was terrifying. Then again, so was the idea of the man in the flat cap catching up with them.

Decision made, Olive sprinted towards the doors, dragging Frankie with her. They launched themselves into the carriage, the doors swept shut behind them, and a moment later the train was off. The children panted and with each heavy breath Olive felt the dawning realisation that they'd just crossed a point of no return. They were now alone in London.

'Poor Howard,' wailed Frankie, gripping on to a pole so as not to stumble.

'Don't worry, he'll be fine. He can handle anything. He's a trained spy, remember?' Olive was sounding much more confident than she felt.

'But what about *us*, Olive? We're not trained spies, in case you've forgotten. What if that man catches up with us?'

Olive sighed. She wished her brother didn't have to articulate every worried thought that crossed her mind. 'He won't,' she said, making her voice sound more confident than she felt. 'We're safe now, Frankie.'

The children both counted the stops carefully. At the seventh stop, as instructed by Howard, they leaped off the train, feeling immense relief not to see the man in the flat cap disembark from one of the other carriages. Hovering next to the escalators, where they could run if needed, they waited for the next train to arrive to see if Howard might be on it, and then the next one. They waited two, five, seven minutes, hoping with every arriving train to see Howard with his brown leather jacket and head of greyish hair, and hoping *not* to see the man in the flat cap.

When it had been ten minutes since their arrival

with not a sign of either man, Olive put a gentle hand on Frankie's shoulder.

'It's time to go.' Her voice was kind. 'Remember what Howard told us. We have to do this, for Grandma Sylvie.'

With a dipped head, Frankie nodded sadly and a few minutes later, they exited the station.

They found themselves in a muggy, grey London afternoon, scented with the aromas of warmed concrete and exhaust fumes. Heading in the direction of the river, they crossed one busy road then another, passing building works and towering skyscrapers. When the riverfront came into view, Olice shaded her eyes to search for spy headquarters. Straight up ahead was a squat stone and glass building that she recognised instantly from the photograph Howard had shown them. It had a blocky appearance, all squares and lines and rectangles, as if the person who'd designed it had been playing a giant game of Tetris.

'There it is!' said Olive, feeling immediately better. 'Now we just need to get somebody's attention, so we can tell them why we're here.'

'But what if they don't listen to us?'

'We'll have to make them. It's a matter of national security, remember?'

Crossing the road, they followed the black iron fencing that ran along the perimeter of the building. A man walked up to the gated entrance and scanned something, then the gates opened and he entered. Olive hurried up to the gate. She gave it a tug, just in case it hadn't closed properly, but it was locked. Then she noticed a police officer standing guard. She was looking the other way and hadn't yet noticed the children. Olive coughed to get her attention.

'Excuse me,' she said politely, 'this might come as a surprise, but we have important information for the British Intelligence Service. We need to talk to Sir Bobbie Eden right away, please.'

The police officer eyed her with disbelief. 'Need to talk to . . .' she repeated, then laughed. 'Do you think I was born yesterday?'

Olive faltered. 'Please, just let us through the gates,' cut in Frankie earnestly, 'and we'll prove we're telling the truth.'

The police officer paused. 'Oh, I get it,' she said after a moment, rolling her eyes. 'You've watched a film or two and now you both want to be *spies*. Well, this isn't a movie or a theme park. It's a very serious place. Go on, go back to your tour group.'

Frankie tried to persuade her next, then Olive had

another go. But no matter what they said, they couldn't get the woman to take them seriously.

After a while, and when the police officer seemed to be losing her patience, the children reluctantly shuffled away.

'What now?' said Frankie anxiously.

Olive, meanwhile, was already sizing up the fence. 'I reckon this fence isn't much higher than the school gates. I think I could make it . . . at a stretch. And if I don't, at least it will get the attention of someone inside. Maybe they'll listen to us. Keep watch for the police officer.'

Frankie, who had seen his sister successfully climb many difficult and unsuitable obstacles throughout their lives, reluctantly nodded. He stared nervously in the direction of the police officer, who at this moment was looking in the opposite direction. The second Olive set her hands on the lowest steel bar, however, the police officer appeared at her side. 'Excuse me,' she said, more bemused than angry, 'what exactly do you think you're doing?'

'You don't understand. We need to get in!' said Olive, jumping back down on to the pavement.

'Do you two even know what this building is? Or how much hot water you could get in for messing around like this?' The police officer's voice was getting louder now. A bead of sweat rolled down Olive's forehead. This felt worse than being told off by one of her teachers. She imagined what their mother would say when she found out that both her children had not only skipped school, but gone to London on their own, tried to break into a government building, and been arrested. But a moment later it appeared her plan had worked, because before she could give the police officer an answer, a voice came from the other side of the fence.

'Olive? Frankie? What are you two doing here?'

Looking through the gaps between the iron bars, Olive saw a woman with grey eyes and curly, red-brown hair staring questioningly down at her. Olive made a choking sound that was both a gasp of surprise and sigh of relief.

'We know her . . . we know her!' shouted Frankie.

The police officer glanced for verification at Agent Nest. 'They do,' she said softly. 'I can chaperone them from here.' Agent Nest walked along the fence and exited through the security gates. The police officer, with a curious glance at the siblings, reluctantly strolled away.

'Let's take a walk by the river where we won't be

overheard,' Agent Nest said as she reached the children. 'Although I don't have long. There's somewhere important I have to be this afternoon.'

Side by side, they strolled along the main road before turning down a set of steps. Then they walked for a few minutes along a tree-lined path that ran parallel to the river. Construction on new skyscrapers was taking place noisily on the street level above, but the path itself was empty. Olive noticed that they hadn't encountered another person for some time. She was bursting to tell Agent Nest about what they'd discovered and how they had been wrong about Howard Sweet, but something about Agent Natasha Nest's brisk, distracted demeanour told her it was best to wait a moment.

'Thanks, Agent Nest,' said Frankie, finally breaking the silence. 'I thought we were in big trouble then.'

'You would have been. What were you thinking? If it were that easy to break into the headquarters of the British Intelligence Service, people would do it all the time.'

'We had to get someone's attention though. We think we've uncovered the identity of Shadow,' Olive blurted out, unable to stop herself. She was immediately cross with herself for not waiting as she'd resolved to, but once she'd started, she figured she might as well tell the agent everything. 'And it's not who we thought! Howard Sweet is innocent.'

'Oh?' Agent Nest stopped and looked at Olive intensely, making Olive feel embarrassed for her sudden outburst. 'That's tremendous work. And who do you think it is?'

'A man named Professor Lachlan Thorn. He founded a company called Forget Me Not, where he records people's memories. Our grandmother recorded her own memories with him . . . only we didn't tell you that part before,' Olive finished guiltily.

'Your grandmother recorded her memories?' Agent Nest's eyes were wide.

'Yes, and Professor Thorn tampered with them to make *her* look guilty instead of him,' Olive answered quickly. We don't know exactly why, but we think he's held a grudge against our grandmother for thirteen years. Ever since—'

'Operation Beehive,' Agent Nest cut in calmly, nodding as if everything they said made perfect sense.

'Exactly!' replied Olive excitedly. 'We know it sounds a bit crazy, but we think we can prove what exactly Professor Thorn has done. And it might not even stop with Grandma. He might be tampering with loads of other people's memories too.'

'My goodness . . . tampering with the memories. That's astonishing work, you two. And where are your grandmother's real memories now?'

Olive reached into Frankie's backpack. 'Right here!' she said, proudly holding aloft the Memoriser.

Agent Nest shook her head slowly. 'May I?' she asked, and Olive handed her the Memoriser. 'I said it yesterday, and I'll say it again. You two would make fantastic spies. I wouldn't be surprised if in a few years I see you two walking the floors of the building behind me. What else have you got in that backpack?'

Olive fought a smile. 'We have these dossiers that our grandmother left us. They helped us work everything out. There's one on Professor Thorn . . .' Olive scrambled to find the file from the bunch, and, in her urgency, she dropped them all.

'You didn't mention these dossiers before either.' Agent Nest reached down to help Olive pick them up. 'Oh, look. There's even a file about me.' She opened it up and laughed. 'Your grandmother really was very thorough. She even knew about my passion for origami.'

Olive opened her mouth, about to tell her all about their journey to London and the man who had been following them, when something stopped her. Looking slowly down at the dossiers, she thought back to the moment they'd first discovered them. *She even likes origami,* her brother had said, reading through Agent Nest's file. At the time, Olive had disregarded the information, believing that Frankie was wasting time with silly details. Suddenly she felt cold, then very hot, all over.

'Origami,' Olive said, more to herself than to Agent Nest. She'd started to feel unsteady on her feet. 'You learnt it as a child.'

Olive was thinking of the memory she'd watched earlier that day. The memory of the man on the phone at the bar, which Howard had mentioned back at the retirement home. Olive could see the two half-empty drinks on the bar and, next to one of them, the napkin folded perfectly into a swan.

'My mother travelled a lot, given her work. Origami was one of my little hobbies,' said Agent Nest. 'Now, thank you for letting me know about your investigation into Professor Thorn. Rest assured that I will take the appropriate action. But at the moment, there's somewhere I need to be, so I'll have to say goodbye to you both.'

Olive ignored her. 'Professor Thorn accidentally

showed us the real memories when Howard was messing around in the archive. I bet he edited out that origami swan in the version he wanted us to see . . .'

'You're babbling now,' said Agent Nest. 'As I said, I really must—'

'When you said you wanted to speak to us yesterday,' Olive cut in, 'it wasn't really because you were concerned about us at all, was it . . . or about Grandma's reputation as a spy . . . You just wanted to find out what we knew about Shadow . . . because . . .'

'Because . . . ?' prompted Agent Nest.

Olive swallowed. Her heart was racing. She looked at Frankie, who judging by his ghost-white face seemed to be coming to the exact same realisation. 'Because *you* are Shadow!'

Agent Nest smiled patiently. 'That's an interesting theory.'

Olive stared at the Memoriser in Agent Nest's hands. 'Give us that back, please.'

At that moment, Olive became aware of somebody else standing near them on the path. Looking across, she saw a man with a flat cap and a dimpled chin. Her heart sank.

'Ah, at last,' said Agent Nest. 'Here he is. Antoine Levigne.'

Frankie gave a squeak of horror. 'You . . . you . . . know each other?'

'Oh, yes,' replied Agent Nest. Her eyes were shining. 'Antoine and I go way back. We met during my years living in France.'

'How could you do this to Grandma Sylvie?' said Olive. 'She trusted you. She was best friends with your mother. She even named me after her . . .'

'Your grandmother wasn't quite the great friend to my mother that she pretended to be.' Agent Nest's voice was still light and quiet but now it had an edge to it. 'She wasn't a great hero, either, though she made everyone believe she was. For years she's made everyone believe Violet Nest was a fool. That she'd made a bad decision and paid the ultimate price. But who do you think was really responsible for my mother's death? Who do you think *suggested* she go to meet that source during Operation Beehive, a meeting which turned out to be a deadly trap?'

'No.' Olive's heart turned to ice. 'Not Grandma Sylvie . . .'

'That's right. Your *legendary* grandmother.'

'Is that why you started stealing secrets from her?' asked Frankie in a small voice. 'Because you blamed her for your mother's death?'

Agent Nest touched the locket around her neck. 'My mother was in hospital for a week before she died from her injuries. In that time, she told me everything. How Sylvie had set her up, how she gave her bad intelligence on purpose. All because Sylvie was tired of being in my mother's shadow all those years. Of course, Sylvie *claimed* it was a mistake, that afterwards she'd told her not to go. But I didn't believe a word of her lies. Instead, I vowed to get revenge.' Agent Nest was now quite unlike the reserved person they'd met the previous day. She didn't seem gentle or bookish any more. Her eyes were flaming with rage, her breathing was heavy. She took a moment to compose herself, smoothing down her curls and straightening her patched-up blazer. When she spoke again, her voice was gentler. 'It just so happened that Professor Lachlan Thorn came to visit my mother in hospital. He'd been working on Operation Beehive and felt terrible that she'd been hurt. If he'd done his job better, then perhaps she would have had the gadgets she needed to protect herself. It was then he told me about his fascinating research into memory. His technology wasn't very advanced at that point. He couldn't get a penny of funding. But it gave me an idea. If I could help him turn his plans into reality, then perhaps Sylvie Jones wouldn't be the only one who could change the past.'

'You convinced – or guilt-tripped – Professor Thorn to leave espionage thirteen years ago,' said Olive, putting the pieces together. 'So he could set up Forget Me Not.'

'Lucky for me,' Agent Nest continued, 'Lachlan Thorn has always been remarkably easy to manipulate. It didn't take too much to convince him to join my plan to take down Sylvie Jones, when I told him what she'd done. It helped, of course, that I gave him the money to set up Forget Me Not. Lots and lots of money, in fact, over the years, which of course I gained by stealing Sylvie's secrets. Two birds . . . one stone. And the rest, as they say, is history. Now –' she clapped her hands together – 'that's enough story time for today. You two should be getting home. As I told you yesterday, this isn't a world your grandmother would have wanted you two to get mixed up in.'

'You're wrong,' Olive said fiercely. 'She trusted us to carry on her mission. She trusted us to help finish what she didn't have the chance to. And that was to stop you!'

'She would have been dreadfully disappointed in that case. Not only have you failed to stop me, but you have also failed to work out what I've been planning all along. My aspirations go far higher than Sylvie Jones. This afternoon marks the start of a special new partnership between Forget Me Not Inc. and the British Intelligence Service. The technology Professor Thorn has developed with my funding is remarkably useful in the espionage business, as it turns out.'

Olive was stunned, barely able to get her words out. 'You'll never get away with it! Not when the Service hears that you've been selling secrets all these years!'

'Ah, but that's the beauty of it, don't you see? We *will* get away with it, because we can make people believe *anything* we want them to. We can edit memories to make it look like your foolish grandmother was a mole, and we're completely innocent. We have the technology to control memories. That means we can control anything we want to.'

'That's terrible,' Olive spat. 'You can't . . . you won't get away with it!'

'But *you* were convinced, weren't you, Olive? When you watched your grandmother's memories, you were ready to believe them. What makes you think other people will be any different?'

'We'll tell them,' said Frankie. 'We'll tell everybody what you're doing.'

'But you have no proof.' Agent Nest laughed, a real laugh this time, nothing like the soft chuckle they'd heard before. 'It's your word against mine. And who would believe a couple of children? The grandchildren of the *deceitful* Sylvie Jones, no less.'

With a sickening feeling, Olive realised that Agent Nest was right. They needed the evidence in the original, undoctored memories to prove what Agent Nest had done – evidence that their grandmother had overlooked, like the origami swan napkin. But Olive had handed them over. How could she have been so stupid? She'd started to feel dizzy, like the world around her was spinning. Everything had gone horribly, irreversibly wrong, and it was all her fault.

Agent Nest checked her watch. 'Now, I really do have to go. Antoine, be a dear, will you, and make sure these two don't cause any more trouble?'

'*Oui*.' He sighed glumly, looking as if he'd rather eat slugs. 'If I must.'

With that, Agent Nest walked over to a set of narrow steps that led directly down to the riverbank. The children rushed to the wall overlooking the river, staring down with horror as they saw what was waiting for her. A shiny red speedboat.

Agent Nest jumped on board and started the engine. Smiling up at the children, she pushed on the accelerator. 'Goodbye, Olive and Frankie Jones!' she shouted over her shoulder as the boat began to speed away. 'I hope you always *remember* this moment!'

# CHAPTER FIFTEEN

# The Gold Watch

Antoine kicked a drinks can that littered the towpath, sending it flying over the wall and on to the riverbank below. 'I don't have time for babysitting,' he snarled as soon as Agent Nest was out of view.

'That's fine by us,' Olive replied fiercely. 'My brother and I will be out of your hair. Come on, Frankie.'

She grabbed her brother's hand and started walking away towards the steps that led back up to the main road, knowing even as she did so that it was never going to be that easy.

'You'd like that, wouldn't you?' Antoine laughed spitefully, moving to block their path. 'Oh no, no, no. I may have better places to be, but you two aren't going anywhere.'

Roughly, he grabbed Olive and Frankie by the

back of their necks and pushed them towards the wooden staircase that led down to the riverbank. They'd no choice but to walk down the steps otherwise they would have fallen down them. They found themselves on the riverbank, a rocky stretch of sand mixed with mud. Olive searched in both directions for somebody to shout to for help, but there was nobody there.

Antoine had taken something that looked like a thin rope from his pocket and was twirling it around his fingers menacingly. A look of pretend curiosity passed over his cruel face. 'Did you know, children, that the water in this river goes up and down, depending on the time of day?'

'Thanks for the geography lesson,' said Olive fiercely, trying not to show that she'd noticed the rope in his hands. 'What's your point?'

'My point, *little girl*, is that the tide is rising right now. Later today, this riverbank will be hidden beneath the murky water of the River Thames. That will happen in about . . . oh, an hour or two. I'll be long gone by then, of course. But you two . . .'

Antoine pushed Frankie behind one of the high vertical wooden posts that stood just in front of the river wall.

'Olive!' Frankie shouted, too surprised to resist.

With a stab of fright, Olive leapt at Antoine frantically. She beat and tore at his back, trying desperately to pull him away from her brother. 'Let go of him! Stop! Stop!'

Antoine withstood Olive's attack with ease. 'Did I mention that I have a black belt in karate?' he said lightly. 'If you don't cooperate, I can always make use of my skills. It would certainly make my life easier.' Olive stepped back in fear.

With Olive under control, Antoine barked at Frankie to raise his arms. Then, taking the rope, he set about tying Frankie's wrists together, so that he was stuck in the shadowy space behind the wooden pillar, staring outwards at the river.

Olive, at a loss at what to do, shut her mouth, and stepped backwards, quietly taking stock of the situation. Not far from where she stood, the yellow-brown sand was darkening with the lapping river water. There was a grimy watermark on the wooden posts where the high tide would eventually reach, at least a metre *above* her brother's head.

When he seemed satisfied the rope around Frankie's wrists was secure, Antoine paused to admire his work. '*Fini*!' he declared. 'Now for your troublemaker sister.'

Frankie's small face tightened with fury. It was a look Olive had never seen her brother give before. With a growl, he gave Antoine a forceful kick in the shin, the kind of bone-breaking kick that a donkey would have boasted to his friends about.

'Arghhh!' moaned Antoine, grabbing his leg. 'Stupid boy . . . stupid boy . . . you'll pay for that!'

Olive, despite her fear, was full of pride for her brave brother, even as Antoine swivelled round to face her with a look of unrestrained fury. 'Stand next to your brother and put your hands in position!' he spat. Olive tried desperately to think of a way out. On the opposite side of the river, cars and red buses heaved by, too far away to notice the terrible scene unfolding across the water. She looked past Antoine and back towards the steps. Olive was quick on her feet and might have got past him to run back up to the pathway, but she couldn't leave Frankie behind. Besides, she hadn't forgotten Antoine's karate skills.

With the most dignified look Olive could muster, she stepped behind the next wooden pillar along from Frankie and placed her arms around it, so that her wrists met on the other side. 'Get on with it, then.' She held up her chin, trying to imagine how her grandmother would have handled such a terrible situation. There was no way the legendary Sylvie Jones would have cried, begged, or shown one ounce of fear when backed into a corner like this. She wouldn't have given Antoine the satisfaction of seeing how scared she was – and Olive couldn't let her little brother see it either.

Antoine sneered, looping the rope around Olive's wrists and pulling tightly, then fastening the ends together in an impossibly tight knot.

'There we are.' Antoine took a step back. 'Get comfortable. Take in the view of the River Thames. Make the most of your last moments alive.'

'You won't get away with this,' snarled Olive.

'But I always get away with things. You'll see.' He loped across the muddy sand and back towards the steps, straightening his hat which had become skewed in the struggle. '*Bonne chance, les enfants!*'

'We don't need luck,' Frankie shouted after him. French was his best subject at school. 'We're the grandchildren of Sylvie Jones!'

*

The shoreline lapped at their feet. Seagulls taunted them from above, flaunting their freedom. Many times, they'd tried wriggling their hands free. At one point Olive had picked up a stray pebble with her foot in case, somehow, she could use it to saw through the rope, but it hadn't worked. The children had tried shouting as loudly as they could, straining their voices until they were hoarse, but that was no use either. The noisy construction works easily drowned them out. Their position behind the wooden posts meant they were hidden both from those walking along the path above and those sailing past on boats.

Exhausted from their efforts, the children rested their foreheads against their pillars. Olive's feet were already soaking wet, and she knew Frankie's must have been too, though neither had mentioned it. Olive had to at least try to keep hope alive. It was her responsibility as the older sister to do so as long as she possibly could. It was also her responsibility, however, to keep her brother alive, and she was doing a terrible job of that, too. It was *her* fault that they were now in mortal danger. She'd been the one who had insisted they take on Mission Shadow, no matter the risk. Olive was always getting carried away and taking things too far. But this time she wasn't the only one facing the consequences.

Olive couldn't bear considering what would happen

when the water got higher, and higher, and higher, as it inevitably would. No, it was too terrible, too horrible, to think about.

Suddenly, as Olive sank lower into despair, Frankie lifted his head from his hands. 'Olive! What about the gadgets?'

'The gadgets . . . ? The gadgets!' she cried. Her heart lifted like it was filled with helium.

'Oh, of course!' Frankie, who was still wearing the backpack, twisted his body so that the bag faced his sister. With difficulty, and straining her neck, she managed to peel back the zip using her teeth. (Their mother often told them not to use their teeth to open things, but Olive was sure this occasion would be an exception.)

'Can you see anything that might help us cut the rope?'

'I can see the tracker pistol, some fake moustaches and the explosive football,' said Olive. 'Nothing that looks like it could set us free.'

Frankie gave an anguished cry. The water was lapping at their ankles now. It wouldn't be long before the water reached their knees.

*This can't be it*, Olive thought. *This can't be how it ends.*

Leaning her head around the pillar, she checked her watch. Was that really the time? Only half an hour had passed since Antoine had left them to die. It had seemed like much longer. Then again, the watch was a little slow.

That moment, she remembered her grandmother's words about the gold watch – *It runs a little slow, but it still has its uses.*

Olive blinked. Staring at the watch, she noticed something. Beneath the clockface was a small gold button, with their grandmother's tiny initials, S.J. How had she missed it before? Straight away it reminded her of the initialled gold button on the armchair in her grandmother's bungalow. When she'd pressed that gold button, something completely unexpected had happened. And something completely unexpected was exactly what she needed right now.

Bracing herself, she nudged the gold button against the wooden pillar. A second later, the ornate clockface folded back to reveal a glowing screen. It looked like the screens in Grandma Sylvie's office, only much smaller. There was a list of options, including INFRARED CAMERA and VOICE RECORDER and LASER BEAM. The last option was ROPE CUTTER.

'Frankie!' she yelped. 'Grandma's watch . . . it . . . it

has . . . a laser . . . and something to cut ropes!'

Frankie's head rose slowly. Seeing the transformed watch, he almost choked with excitement. 'No way! Do you think you can make it work?'

Olive's heart raced. She suspected that the watch would be voice activated just like her grandmother's car, now she'd pressed the gold button. 'Yes, I think I can,' she told her brother, closing her eyes and taking a breath.

'Gold watch,' Olive said a little uncertainly, not knowing whether that was the right way to address it. 'Activate ROPE CUTTER.' Instantly, the glowing screen lifted. A flat blade slid slowly from beneath it and, without touching her skin, extended towards the rope, before slicing clean through it, and then folding back into the watch face. For a few seconds, she blinked in confusion. She'd done it. Her hand was free!

Olive quickly shook off the bind. Stepping away from the wooden pillar, she gave a cry of triumph. Then, with her hands now free, Olive quickly set about untying Frankie.

The very first thing he did with his regained freedom was to wrap his arms tightly around his sister, his chest heaving with a sob. Relief flooded through Olive like an antidote. It was so strong and instant that it sent tears rolling down her cheeks. The siblings stood there for a moment, both of their feet submerged in the water, before Olive felt her brother's grip loosen. She pressed the button, to restore the gold watch to its former appearance. Then they scrambled towards the steps that led away from the water, relieved beyond words to reach the path above.

'I thought we were really going to run out of time then . . .' Frankie wiped away tears and rubbed at the red marks on his wrists.

'It's OK now,' she said gently. 'We're safe.'

The children hurried down the path back towards the street. When they saw a figure in the distance Olive's first terrified thought was that Antoine was back. Then she saw the brown bomber jacket and greyish hair of Howard Sweet. He looked as if he'd aged a decade with worry.

'Where on earth have you been?' he demanded as he reached them. 'I've been looking everywhere for you.'

'Howard!' Frankie squeaked, and they both threw their arms around him.

Olive explained everything that had happened since they'd been separated. Howard's face turned purple with rage when she told them how Antoine had left them tied to the pillars. When she'd finished the story, he gave her an impressed look. 'Well done, Olive. Sylvie Jones herself would have been proud of such a daring escape.'

Olive blushed. Compliments always made her insides squirm and her cheeks go hot. She moved the conversation on to more important matters. 'How are we going to stop Agent Nest and Professor Thorn now though? We don't even know where she was going!'

'I have a pretty good idea about that.' Howard's eyes narrowed. 'There's a hotel in Westminster called St Barbary's. The intelligence service uses the top two floors as a place away from headquarters to meet and share top-secret information. My sources tell me there's a meeting there today. I'm almost certain that's where she went.'

'But . . . can we get there in time?' Olive asked. 'Agent Nest left on a speedboat almost an hour ago now.'

Howard pursed his lips. 'In this city, there's only one mode of transport that's faster than travelling by water.'

'What?' asked the children in unison.

Craning his neck backwards, Howard looked up at the clouds above. His face showed the beginnings of a smile.

# CHAPTER SIXTEEN

# St Barbary's Hotel

'I shouldn't have made a copy of the key, of course.' Howard reached into his jacket pocket. 'But I had a feeling having access to this place might one day come in handy.'

They were standing in front of a tall brick building, several storeys high, with a closed garage door at the front and a sign that read 'HAND CAR WASH AND VALETING'. Stuck on to the front of the garage door was yet another sign, which this time read 'GONE FOR LUNCH – BACK SOON', even though it was now closer to dinner time.

Howard jostled the key in the rusted padlock. Behind his back, the children shared a doubtful look. They knew by now not to judge anything by its appearance – a lesson from their grandmother that neither would ever forget – but this place seemed to test that wisdom. A few seconds later, there was a noise like a spring releasing and the door opened.

Howard pushed inside. 'Come on. Straight to the top!'

The children followed him up a concrete staircase, one flight of stairs and then another, and another, and another. Olive was soon out of breath, but Howard powered on.

'Come on, a few flights of stairs won't kill you!' he called back to them. 'In my lifetime, I've summited many of the toughest mountains in the world! The mighty Mount Kilimanjaro in Tanzania . . . the exquisite Khüiten Peak in Mongolia . . . the wondrous Mount Elbrus in Russia . . . the glorious Annapurna in Nepal. Two of those were with your grandmother!'

Olive tried to picture her grandmother climbing a mountain and picked up her pace, resolving that one day she'd climb those mountains too.

The staircase led to a bare concrete landing with a grimy door. Following Howard through, the children found themselves standing outside on a flat and square roof. It was unremarkable in every way, except for what was sitting at its centre. Olive and Frankie stared, open-mouthed.

It was a helicopter. Bigger than Olive would've ever imagined, with a rounded metallic blue body and a set of four blades at the top, it looked like an overgrown beetle. Her stomach flipped at the thought of lifting off from the roof in its belly.

'Hope you two aren't scared of heights!' Howard shouted over the noise of the wind whipping across the rooftop. He slid the helicopter's door open.

'No way!' Olive shouted back, too proud to let her nerves show.

'Can you fly a helicopter, Howard?' asked Frankie.

'Of course I can! So could your grandmother,' he scoffed. 'Although, these days the helicopters fly themselves!'

Having spent the last two days in a driverless car, this idea didn't sound as ridiculous to Olive as it might have done before.

Howard jumped on board as casually as if he were getting into a car. Olive and Frankie followed. Like in the driverless car, there was no steering wheel or cockpit or controls, just circular, bench-style seating built into the sides of the helicopter. The door automatically slid shut after them and the children took their seats, buckling heavy seatbelts across their shoulders.

'Helicopter 0102, this is Captain Howard Sweet. Take us to St Barbary's Hotel, fast as you can.'

'*Destination confirmed*,' replied a polite robotic voice. '*Please prepare for take-off.*'

'Ready yourselves!' shouted Howard to the children, as if addressing soldiers under his command. 'We're outta here!'

The helicopter began to vibrate. '*For your safety, please remain seated*,' the robotic voice continued. '*We hope your short trip is enjoyable. Don't forget to enjoy the view!*'

Olive looked over at Frankie, who was holding on to his seatbelt so tightly his knuckles were white. She closed her eyes and took a deep breath, trying to steady her nerves. By the time she opened them again and had built up the courage to peer out of the window, the helicopter had risen several metres from the roof and was ascending rapidly. Within seconds, they were so high off the ground that the city below looked like a toy town. Then, with a gliding motion, they zoomed away from the rooftop.

Olive could see that they were following the path of the river below. Somehow this settled her nerves. Strangely, seeing the water from above like that made Olive think of her grandmother. On the surface, the elderly lady had always seemed cold, distant, unreachable, much like the icy-looking river. But underneath the surface, Olive now knew, she had been extraordinary. Hidden behind her stony exterior was a mind that fizzed with brilliance. Grandma Sylvie had lived her life at the extremes, showing remarkable spirit and courage in the face of danger. She'd seen places in the world Olive had only read about in books. And she'd achieved things nobody else had. Over the past few days, Olive had been able to glimpse beneath the surface at the person her grandmother had been. But she knew that it was only a glimpse. Like the river rolling out beneath her, there was more, so much more, to her grandmother than she'd ever know.

'We'll be there in two minutes,' shouted Howard over the noise of the helicopter, drawing Olive away from her thoughts. Frankie groaned; now they were in the air he clearly didn't want the ride to end.

They were already getting lower in the sky. Then the helicopter hovered in place, before lowering jerkily downwards, tipping left and right, towards a circular launch pad below. When they finally touched down, Olive let out her breath through gritted teeth. They heard the rotating blades above gradually slow, and vibration of the engine stopped.

Without a moment's pause, Howard Sweet unbuckled his seatbelt. 'No time to delay!' he urged. He leaped out of the helicopter, on to the roof of St Barbary's Hotel.

As soon as her legs would cooperate, Olive followed his lead, then turned to help Frankie down. She was relieved to be on solid ground again, even if the location was as precarious as a rooftop.

Howard Sweet led the way across the roof towards a door. He paused at the sight of a padlock, cursing in frustration when he found the key didn't fit. 'They must have changed the lock.'

Olive stepped forwards, smiling. 'Allow me,' she said, pressing the gold button on her grandmother's watch. She'd been hoping she'd have a chance to use one of its other functions. 'Gold watch, activate laser,' she said, directing the watch towards the padlock. A blue beam shone from the clockface, slicing through the metal with ease and sending the padlock clattering to the floor. Olive looked back at Howard Sweet.

'Not bad work for a novice,' he said with a smile.

She beamed proudly as she pushed open the unlocked door. They stepped into a gold carpeted hallway with ornate lamps and paintings of racehorses on the walls. Olive looked down at her shoes, soggy with river water, and those of her brother's. Both were muddying the plush carpet. When Howard had told them about St Barbary's Hotel, Olive had imagined the kind of hotel she had stayed at on family holidays. She'd pictured lots of important spies crammed into a tiny room with twin beds and scratchy blankets. It had seemed like an odd location for such important business to be conducted. But *this* kind of hotel, the *very*, *very* posh kind, where afternoon tea is served on pretty silver trays and smartly uniformed people open the doors for guests as they arrive, made much more sense.

Howard set off down the stairs. 'We need to go to the kitchen first,' he said, keeping his voice hushed. 'It's in the basement.'

Olive frowned with confusion. 'I thought you said the meetings were on the top two floors?'

'I did,' replied Howard, 'but we can't just barge in through the main doors, can we? Our best chance of getting into the room undetected is to go in disguise.'

And so down the stairs they ran. After ten floors, they reached a sign marked LOBBY. They kept going. On the next floor was a sign marked SPA AND SWIMMING POOL, and then on the next, one marked CINEMA. Finally, they came to a sign which read KITCHEN – STAFF ONLY.

They pushed through the door into a hot, frenetic place of shiny metal appliances and bubbling pans, so busy with activity that nobody paid the slightest attention to three newcomers. A woman who had to be the head chef, dressed smartly in a white coat with a matching hat, was expertly shaking a flaming pan with one hand while stirring a saucepan with the other.

'Salmon ready for garnish! And what's taking so long with the sauce?' she yelled.

Howard marched across the tiled floor, giving off an air of being exactly where he belonged, straight to where two white coats were hanging on hooks. Without an ounce of hesitation, he grabbed them and strolled back to the children.

'Put these on.' He threw one coat to Olive and another to Frankie. 'And hold these.' He whipped two silver trays from the sideboard and shoved them into the children's hands. Then he took two glass dishes of prawns, filled them with a mysterious green sauce that was bubbling on the hob, and placed the dishes on to Olive and Frankie's trays. 'Let's call them prawn cocktails,' he said. 'The service lift is over there. Off you go!'

'Aren't you coming?' asked Olive, panicking.

'Of course, I just need to find another coat . . .' he said. 'I'll join you shortly. Go!'

The trays of prawn cocktail (which until then Olive had known only as a crisp flavour) wobbled on Olive and Frankie's trays as they hurried across the room. They were halfway across the kitchen when they heard a shout.

'Excuse me . . . who are you?' a voice yelled.

The children turned to see the head chef, flaming pan in hand, looking furiously at Howard. Without missing a beat, Howard bent over slightly, a grimace appearing on his face. 'Ah,' he moaned, sounding suddenly very frail and weak. 'Thank goodness you found me. I'm terribly lost!' He looked around, blinking, as if seeing a kitchen for the very first time. Just then, the service lift doors opened. Howard turned to them and mouthed, 'Go!'

'Somebody help this poor gentleman!' the chef – once again – yelled. 'Then get him *out* of my kitchen! *And tell me where my sauce is!*'

Olive and Frankie hurried into the lift just as the doors closed, unseen by the chefs in the kitchen who were frantically looking for the missing sauce.

The lift was old and rickety. The glass dishes of prawns rattled against the silver trays as the lift journeyed upwards.

'What are we going to do now?' moaned Frankie.

'We'll just have to work it out as we go along,' said Olive, who was by now gaining in confidence.

When the doors opened at the top, Olive and Frankie stepped cautiously out into a narrow, empty lobby with a double doorway at the far end. The doors were ajar and voices were floating through the opening.

Olive rushed to the double doors and peeked through the crack. Inside she saw a large, elegant space filled with well-dressed adults milling around a bar. At the far end of the room was another set of double doors which were open. Olive could see that beyond was *another* room with a long conference table and high windows half-covered by thick red velvet curtains.

'This must be the meeting,' whispered Olive. 'But we won't be able to hear properly from here. We need to get inside, so we can listen in and hear what Agent Nest is up to. Ready, Frankie?'

'Ready.' He adjusted his white coat, which, though he was tall for his age, was so big for him it almost dragged along the floor.

Olive straightened her back and lifted her chin into

the air, balancing the silver tray on her palm. Frankie, catching on, did the same. Leading the way, Olive strode confidently through the double doors and into the room of chattering spies. To her surprise, she lost dishes of prawn cocktail as she passed through the crowd, with requests for 'more canapés please' and 'vegetarian options next time'. At first Olive was worried somebody might stop them when they noticed they were only children, but she needn't have worried. The spies weren't in the least bit interested in who was serving the prawns, only that they got a dish before they ran out.

Reaching the doors to the room with the large conference table in it, they slid their now empty silver trays behind a cabinet. Then, when sure nobody was watching, they slipped through to the next room, looking for somewhere to hide.

'*We're ready to begin*,' a voice announced from the bar in the other room, which was followed by the shuffle of feet in their direction.

Panicked, Olive caught Frankie's eye and pointed at the red velvet curtains. The children hurried behind the thick, plush fabric just in time, Olive behind one curtain and Frankie behind another. A second later, they heard people filing into the room.

Peeking out from behind her curtain, Olive saw spies in smart clothes pouring themselves glasses of water or cups of tea before taking seats around the large, oval table. When she spotted Agent Nest making her way to the front of the room, Olive's whole body tensed. It took every bit of restraint she possessed not to charge out from behind the curtain and launch herself at the woman. Instead, she thought of every horrible thing she could imagine and wished they would all happen to Agent Nest at once.

'Shall we begin?' Agent Nest addressed the room amiably, unaware of the many terrible fates being wished for her, only metres away. 'As some of you know, today marks the start of an exciting new approach for the British Intelligence Service. The revolutionary memory technology developed by Forget Me Not Inc. will herald a new era in our intelligence work.'

There was a polite round of applause. Agent Nest clapped her hands too, smiling at a man sitting at the opposite end of table. With another powerful surge of anger, Olive saw that it was none other than Professor Lachlan Thorn.

'Memory,' continued Agent Nest, 'has always been of the utmost importance in our industry. Agents have thorough training to ensure they can retain information with the highest possible degree of accuracy, whether that be a top-secret location, or a code, or a name. This is crucial for the success of our work – and for the safety of the public. And yet agents are only human. Sometimes mistakes happen. Sometimes memory fails us. And that's where the Memoriser comes in.'

Agent Nest paused, holding up a white object which Olive recognised immediately. Olive could tell from the reactions in the room that while some also recognised the object, others were clearly seeing it for the first time.

'The revolutionary technology contained within this extraordinary device will allow agents to record their memories and for authorised users to watch them back afterwards. It can be used to re-examine events and spot important information that agents might have initially missed. It can also be used to double-check stories that might not quite add up. In short, the Memorisers will transform our intelligence capabilities, for ever.'

There was a second round of applause, more enthusiastic this time. Hiding behind the curtain, Olive was seething with rage. She longed to jump out and confront Agent Nest. *Not yet*, she told herself, *wait for the right moment*.

'The technology,' continued Agent Nest, 'was developed by a remarkable scientist who we're lucky enough to have sitting among us this afternoon. Welcome back to the British Intelligence Service, Professor Lachlan Thorn.'

Professor Thorn waved modestly. Then he opened a white briefcase which was sitting on the table in front of him, revealing a stash of shining Memorisers. 'There's one for you all to take home today,' he said. 'You can start storing your memories from the very moment you leave this room.'

At this, there were excited noises from the spies around the table.

'That is, if *you* give us the final go-ahead, sir,' Agent Nest added respectfully, speaking to a slight man sitting at the far side of the table. He was slouching in his chair and had the unmistakable air of being the most important person in the room. Olive guessed that he must be Sir Bobbie Eden, the Chief of the British Intelligence Service.

'My concern is security,' he declared in a grumbly kind of voice. 'If this thing got into the wrong hands . . .'

Olive felt like rushing out from the curtain then

and telling Sir Bobbie Eden that he was right to be concerned. That the Memoriser was *already* in the wrong hands. But something told her . . . *stay where you are a little longer.*

'Rest assured,' replied Agent Nest, 'the best minds in the country have worked around the clock to make sure that only the owners of the memories and their authorised users are able to access the memories stored on the Memoriser.'

Olive was boiling with rage. She couldn't stand the lies. The Memorisers *weren't* secure. And what's more, Professor Thorn had worked out how to alter memories.

'Thank you, Agent Nest. I read your report. And I found it very thorough . . . very impressive,' mumbled Sir Bobbie Eden. 'Very impressive, indeed. Security is still a worry, however.' He paused thoughtfully. 'And of course, if we do sanction these,' he went on, 'officially nobody could know about it. It couldn't go on any records. We'll deny all association with these . . . Memorisers . . . if anyone ever enquires.'

'Quite right, sir.' Agent Nest nodded seriously. Sir Bobbie Eden tapped his fingers on the table, looking to be on the edge of making a decision. Agent Nest walked slowly closer to him, like a predator about to close in on her prey. 'You should know, sir, that three other countries are close to having breakthroughs in their own memory research. No doubt, they'll soon have their own versions of the Memoriser technology. But if we move fast, we can be the first. Otherwise, I fear we'll get left behind.'

'Left behind? No, no, no,' replied Sir Bobbie Eden. 'We must lead the pack!'

'Precisely my thoughts, sir.'

'In that case,' he began, 'begin implementation straight away!' He looked disapprovingly at the suitcase in front of Professor Thorn. 'We'll need a lot more than you have there, Professor. Every agent in the field should have a Memoriser by the end of the week.'

'Excellent, sir.' Agent Nest smiled modestly. 'Can you manage it, Professor Thorn?'

'Certainly,' boasted Professor Thorn.

'Then it's decided.' Sir Bobbie Eden thumped his fist on the table. After a moment, his brow furrowed. 'Now, there's one final piece of business we should attend to before we finish, and I'm afraid it's rather unpleasant. We've long suspected that a mole was operating within our ranks. I'm sorry to say we were correct. It was none other than Sylvie Jones, someone who I'd long thought to be one of the finest agents the business had even seen. Sadly, that was not the case. She was operating with the help of her lawyer, Edith Lowry, who many of us will know. What a disgrace . . . what a shame . . .' He shook his head. 'Going forwards, we'll need to carefully re-examine Sylvie's operations, check any sources she worked with, and so on. We were planning to give her a posthumous award for outstanding service and courage, which of course we no longer will. As for Ms Lowry, we're working on tracking her down and, as soon as we do, she'll be arrested.' There was a moment of discussion around the room. When it died down, Sir Bobbie Eden rose from his chair. 'Now that awful business is dealt with, tell me, are there any more of those prawn canapés? The sauce was unusual but quite delicious.'

In her hiding place, Olive was shaking with anger; if any of the spies had looked over at that exact moment, they would have seen the velvet curtain twitching. She couldn't allow her grandmother to take the blame. She couldn't let Agent Nest and Professor Thorn get away with their horrible plan. She couldn't bear keeping silent for another second while their lies went unchallenged. *It's time*, she thought, *time to put an end to this*.

'Stop!' Olive stepped out from the curtain. 'You

246

don't understand what you're doing!'

Heads turned wildly and chairs shot backwards. *Who? What? How?* came cries from around the room. Olive, meanwhile, was focused only on Agent Nest, who looked stunned.

'Agent Natasha Nest can't be trusted . . . and neither can he!' Olive pointed a shaky finger at Professor Lachlan Thorn, who almost spat out a mouthful of coffee. Olive took a deep breath. Every pair of eyes in the room was directed her way.

'This is outrageous.' Agent Nest laughed incredulously. 'Can somebody kindly remove this child? How has she been allowed to enter here? Are we not the British Intelligence Service?'

Olive persisted. 'Professor Thorn and Agent Nest are planning to use these Memorisers to steal information from the British Intelligence Service. And they can manipulate memories too – for their own good.'

'Lies,' Agent Nest said quickly, shaking her head as if hearing the ramblings of a toddler. 'We don't have time to listen to such fanciful *nonsense*.'

Olive ignored her. 'Please, you have to listen!' she addressed the rest of the room. 'Agent Nest stole intelligence from our grandmother for years. Then she tried to frame her as the mole. When it's been Agent Nest all along!'

Outrage spread through the room. Sir Bobbie Eden had a startled look on his reddening face, as if he was choking on something and unable to speak. Olive could tell very easily when adults didn't believe her – it happened so often after all. And as she searched the faces of the spies around the table, Olive knew she had failed to convince them. On some faces she saw shock, on others anger. But she didn't see any signs that even one of them believed her. The only person in the room not staring right at her was Professor Thorn, who had quietly closed his suitcase of Memorisers and was looking at the door.

'It's the truth.' Frankie spoke in a quiet but steady voice, stepping out from his hiding place. He was visibly shaking with fear. 'You *have* to listen to my sister.'

As the room erupted in response to Frankie's appearance, Olive stared at her brother. She was grateful beyond words. She'd never had anyone back her up like that before. Normally she stood alone before the glare of disbelieving eyes. And she knew how terrifying he'd have found addressing a room of adults like that. Olive had been silly to be jealous of her brother before. Their differences were what made them such a great team, she could see that now. She reached out and took his hand; no matter what happened next, they had each other.

'These two are the grandchildren of the disgraced Sylvie Jones,' said Agent Nest, more calmly now that it was clear no one believed Olive's words. 'She betrayed us over years – probably decades – though I don't need to remind you about that. We have seen the evidence in her memories. They think she was some kind of hero . . . bless them. Clearly, they're delusional. Now, Margaret, please take them away.'

A woman wearing a dark suit stepped forward. She had muscly arms the size of tree trunks and the alert, probing eyes of a security guard. She took Olive and Frankie firmly by the shoulders and started leading them away. 'You're making a huge mistake,' Olive shouted, resisting with all her strength.

'Stop your drivel,' hissed Agent Nest. 'You're nothing more than a child with an overactive imagination!'

'No,' came a steady voice from the double doorway at the end of the room. 'Her imagination is *not* overactive. In fact, it's her greatest asset. It's what has allowed her to work out your terrible plan.'

All the heads in the room turned. A woman wearing a burnt orange blouse was standing in the open doorway, her fierce eyes glaring straight at Agent Natasha Nest.

# CHAPTER SEVENTEEN

## Leap of Faith

An electric tension hung in the air. Murmurs of *Sylvie Jones, Sylvie Jones, Sylvie Jones* rippled across the room until it sounded like the hiss of a serpent.

Grandma Sylvie moved slowly towards the conference table, clearly savouring every single second.

For once, Olive was speechless. Her throat was tight, mouth hanging open. It was as if she'd forgotten all her words. Grandma Sylvie, meanwhile, addressed the room. 'Every word – every single word – my granddaughter has said is absolutely true.'

Agent Nest looked as terrified as if she were talking to a ghost. 'But you're . . .'

'Dead?' said Grandma Sylvie flatly. 'Not last time I checked.'

'Sylvie Jones,' said Sir Bobbie Eden, who was now

no longer red but a kind of purple colour. 'What on earth is going on?'

'She's as deceitful as ever.' Agent Nest's eyes were bright and wide, like those of an animal caught in a trap. 'Even about her own death. We all know your secret, Sylvie. That you were – *are* – a mole.'

'No.' Grandma Sylvie spoke calmly. 'You would like our colleagues to believe that. But it is in fact *you* who is a mole, Natasha Nest. For thirteen years you've stolen classified information from me, putting countless operations – and lives – at risk. But that ends today. Thanks to my grandchildren.'

'How dare you!' Agent Nest cried.

Grandma Sylvie turned to Olive, who stepped backwards with alarm. She'd been watching the spectacle of her grandmother addressing Agent Nest as if it were a programme on television. None of it felt real. *Grandma Sylvie is alive. Grandma Sylvie is alive.* This sentence ran over and over in her head, though it didn't help the truth of the matter to sink in. 'Tell them what you discovered,' prompted Grandma Sylvie. 'You have their attention now.'

With difficulty, Olive swallowed. Somehow, she found the strength to conjure her voice. 'Agent Nest . . . Agent Nest . . .' she spluttered, 'has made loads of money selling secrets she's stolen from Grandma Sylvie. And she used that money to fund Professor Thorn's research at Forget Me Not.'

Agent Nest scoffed. 'Where's the evidence of that?'

Olive opened her mouth, then closed it. The origami swan had seemed like a brilliant clue earlier. It had led Olive to the realisation that Agent Nest was Shadow and prompted Agent Nest to confess. But now it didn't seem nearly enough. And anyway, only Agent Nest had the undoctored memories. She was hardly going to hand those over. Olive needed more proof.

Frankie took a cautious step forward. 'Olive,' he whispered, 'show them the photo on your phone.'

Olive was confused for a second.

'A – N – N . . .' he prompted.

Then she remembered – the photo she'd taken in Professor Thorn's office – the mysterious 'Ann'. With a thrill she worked out what her brother obviously had done already. Quickly, she got the photo up on her phone, holding it out as her brother had instructed.

'This photo shows a bank transfer to Forget Me Not from somebody called Ann,' Frankie explained. 'Or at least that's what we thought before. But Ann isn't really a name; it's a set of initials . . . *Your* initials, Agent Natasha Nest.'

Olive beamed at her brother, prouder than she'd ever been. Agent Nest, meanwhile, tilted her head backwards with a laugh, as if she'd just heard the world's most ridiculous joke. 'How sweet,' she said, 'but I'm afraid that blurry photo proves nothing.'

'We also know your motive,' said Olive. 'You wanted revenge against Grandma Sylvie for the death of your mother, Violet, thirteen years ago.'

Agent Nest's laughter faded. Olive saw what looked like a flash of pain cross her face. 'That's nonsense. Sylvie and my mother were great friends. And Sylvie and I became good friends ourselves. I've admired Sylvie's work since I was a child.' Agent Nest's eyes narrowed. 'Little did I know it was the work of a traitor.'

'You were never really her friend, not since your mother's death. You only wanted to get close to her so you could steal secrets,' Olive shot back. There was a shift in the room. She could tell by their questioning looks that some of the agents were starting to doubt Agent Nest – and to believe Olive.

Agent Nest glowered at the children. 'Natasha,' said Grandma Sylvie. 'Is it true? How could you blame me for your mother's death? You know I tried to save her life.'

'I think I can answer that,' Olive cut in. 'Agent Nest thinks you told her mother to go to the meeting that led to her death on purpose. She thinks you're the reason her mother died.'

'She *is* the reason my mother died.' Agent Nest's voice was eerily quiet.

The room was gripped by silence. Agent Nest had closed her eyes and was breathing heavily. She was letting down her cover, revealing too much.

'Natasha,' said Grandma Sylvie, dumbfounded. 'I never betrayed your mother. Yes, I told her about the new source. And yes, at first I thought they might have had valuable intelligence. But after further investigation, something just didn't feel right. I tried to convince Violet *not* to go to meet them. Your mother wouldn't listen. *That's* the truth. I would have never hurt her.'

'Lies!' screamed Agent Nest, sending a ripple of shock around the room. 'My mother did nothing wrong. Except for trusting *you*. You saw her merely as a rival on your way to the top. You tricked her!'

'That's enough, Agent Nest!' Sir Bobbie Eden had apparently recovered the ability to speak. 'I'd like to know exactly what's going on here. Explain yourself!'

Agent Nest opened her mouth, as if to continue

denying the accusations against her. Then she stopped. She shook her head. Something strange had happened to her features, as if she'd taken off a mask and revealed her true face. 'I can see that you're all still eager to believe in the *legendary Sylvie Jones*. There's nothing I can do to convince you otherwise. And I'm tired of trying to. But I won't stand here any longer and listen to her lies.' She stared hatefully at Grandma Sylvie for a moment, before turning to Sir Bobbie Eden. 'Besides, if the British Intelligence Service doesn't want the Memoriser technology, I can easily take it elsewhere. As I said before, several countries are trying to develop technology of this kind. They'll pay a good price to get their hands on this little machine, so they can figure out how it works and develop their own version.' She held up the Memoriser containing Grandma Sylvie's memories.

'Natasha,' said Grandma Sylvie. 'You've betrayed your country countless times as Shadow. But it's over now. Hand yourself in.'

That moment, Olive noticed Professor Thorn. He had got to his feet during the commotion and was heading towards the door. '*You* can't take the technology *anywhere*.' He was staring at Agent Nest furiously. 'It's *my* invention.'

'My days of helping you are over, Lachlan,' shot back Agent Nest. 'You may wish to go to prison, but I certainly don't. This machine only exists because I helped to fund your research. It's time I was rewarded for my generosity.' Then, too quick even for a room full of spies, she launched herself towards one of the high windows, threw it open and climbed out on to the balcony – then swung herself over the edge. Olive was the first to rush to the window. Agent Nest had landed on the balcony below and was already climbing down to the next.

'Go after her!' shouted Sir Bobbie Eden.

Olive made as if to follow her out of the window but felt a hand on her shoulder. 'I didn't mean you, young lady,' he said. 'Leave this part to the trained agents and police officers.'

Hearing this, Olive clenched her fist. She couldn't let Agent Nest get away again. She glanced at Grandma Sylvie, who gave her a small nod.

That was all the encouragement she needed. Olive quickly assessed her options. She would have liked to use the helicopter to chase Agent Nest, but Howard had the key, and she didn't know where he'd got to. She reckoned if Agent Nest could climb over the balcony and down the building then she could too.

She'd raised her leg up to the window ledge, when she felt Grandma Sylvie's hand on her shoulder.

'I'd take the service lift if I were you,' she said, an amused look on her face. 'Not quite as exciting, but much faster. It comes out at the bins, right by the riverfront.'

Secretly a bit relieved she wouldn't have to scale the building, Olive nodded. 'Come on, Frankie!'

They called the lift and as soon as it arrived and the doors opened they rushed inside. After a few seconds spent hammering the buttons, the lift descended. The moment the doors reponed, Olive and Frankie dashed out, heading for the exit opposite marked STAFF ONLY – WASTE MANAGEMENT. Running outside, they sprinted through the alleyway past rows of bins, turning left when they reached the end. A few steps further and they were at the riverfront, just as Grandma Sylvie had advised. Rushing to the river wall, Olive scanned the scattering of boats docked at a pontoon below. She soon spotted what she was looking for. A red speedboat. And running down a ramp towards it a little way off, almost at the pontoon, was Agent Natasha Nest.

'There she is!' Olive called to Frankie. 'Let's go!'

They set off along the river wall in the direction of

the ramp. Olive had never run so fast in her life. She was sure her pace would have set a new school sprinting record had there been someone around to record it. Even so, by the time they arrived at the top of the ramp, Agent Nest was already on the pontoon and metres away from her boat.

Frankie arrived behind her, panting. 'She's getting away!'

Olive scanned the river desperately, searching for options. Directly below them, people were shuffling on to a tourist boat, the kind that stops along the river at all the city's best attractions. Marked across its side were the words CITY SIGHTS CRUISE. Watching people pile on to the boat, Olive had an idea. The idea was ever so slightly absurd. It was the kind of fanciful escapade Olive's imagination would cook up when she was staring into space in lessons at school. She was about to tell herself to stop being foolish when she remembered what her grandmother had said moments before – about how her imagination was her greatest asset. Hearing those words in her head, Olive started to believe them. Maybe her powerful imagination wasn't something to be sorry about. Maybe her tendency to get lost in her thoughts was something to be celebrated. It was brave to be a dreamer. It made her limitless. And maybe this time she could do more than imagine. She could make it really happen too.

'Frankie.' Olive started down the ramp, gesturing for her brother to follow. 'I don't have time to explain, so you're going to need to trust me here.'

To Frankie's obvious surprise, Olive was heading straight towards the tourist boat. She weaved her way through the small crowd still waiting to board, dragging Frankie behind her. When she got to the ticket person, she told the man a lie about their parents already being on the boat. To her relief, he was distracted by a football game on his mobile phone and waved them on without saying so much as a word.

Olive waited impatiently for the rest of the passengers to board and for the boat to pull away to put the next stage of her plan into action. She climbed up on to one of the seats at the centre of the boat. Clearing her throat, she began with a shout, 'Excuse me, everyone. We need your attention!'

At first, nobody paid her the slightest bit of notice. They were too busy taking selfies or snapping pictures of the grey office buildings along the river front. Olive tried again, even louder. This time, a few people noticed, but rather than paying attention, they eyed her suspiciously and moved further away. Olive sighed, and gave a long, loud wolf-whistle.

'What's that girl doing?' she heard somebody ask. 'Get her off the seat!'

'Whose kid is that misbehaving?' another person shouted.

Now, she had the attention of several passengers, but if she wanted to keep it, she had to cut to the chase. 'I'm sorry to interrupt your trip. My brother and I are working with the British Intelligence Service and we need your help.'

Standing on the deck beneath her, Frankie gave a shy wave. The looks they got in return ranged from bemusement to anger to impatience. 'You two, spies?' scoffed a man near the front. He was wearing a T-shirt with I LOVE LONDON on it. 'That's a nice story, kid. Now get down.'

'Sir,' began Olive steadily, 'we may only be children, but the safety of everybody in the country is resting on our shoulders. And now on yours too.'

'Is this some kind of live-action entertainment?' asked a passenger with a German accent. 'I don't remember it being on the leaflet.'

'No,' Olive replied with exasperation. 'This is very real. And we're running out of time.'

'Well, what is it?' asked a woman impatiently. She was wrestling with a fidgety toddler. 'What do you want us to do?'

'We need help chasing after a dangerous woman. She's wanted by British Intelligence. And she just left in a red speedboat, going in that direction. If she gets away, it will have serious repercussions for national security.'

'I don't have time for this,' another woman shouted. 'We have tickets for the London Eye! We've come all the way from Florida to ride it.'

'Forget the London Eye,' said a man in a bright shirt and striped shorts. 'We have tickets for a show! Three rows back from the stage. They cost an arm and a leg.'

'What's going on back here?' At last the captain emerged from the cabin at the front of the boat. Seeing Olive standing on the chair, he sighed. 'Get that child off there, please.'

'Captain, thank *goodness*!' said the woman from Florida with a warm smile. 'These children want us to follow some boat down the river. Apparently, it's a matter of national security.'

'A matter of *what*?' replied the captain incredulously, not returning the Floridian woman's smile or warmth.

He clearly had to deal with his fair share of nonsense as captain of the CITY SIGHTS CRUISE and had no appetite for more. 'Whoever is responsible for these children, please get them under control!'

In response, the crowd gave a murmur of approval. Olive sensed the crowd's attention starting to wander back to selfies. Olive and Frankie shared a worried look.

'I believe them!' came a shout from somewhere in the crowd. A young boy with glasses, about Frankie's age, had climbed up on to a seat too. 'Look,' he shouted, 'you can see the red boat up ahead! They really are spies.'

'I believe them too!' said a young girl of around seven, also now standing on a seat. 'We have to help!'

'Me too!' said the child of the Floridian woman.

'And me!' shouted another.

There was a group of around twenty children on a school trip, and at that moment they all rose to their feet and turned on their teachers. 'We have to help!' Olive heard one of them say. 'Yeah, we have to!' said another. 'Didn't you hear? It's a matter of national security!'

Very soon, every single child on the boat was pleading with the adults around them. The noise cut straight through the rushing wind and the sound of the engine. Olive got down from her seat, with an encouraging nod from her brother, and strode straight up to the front of the boat.

'Captain,' she shouted above the noise, 'we're going to need to increase our speed to the maximum if we're to catch the red boat.' When he didn't move, a child next to him, one of the first to have spoken up, tapped him politely on the shoulder. 'Please, Captain!' she said. 'As fast as you can!'

'I think you'd better, captain!' said one woman, a mother of two boys who had been particularly ardent in their support. 'If the children are right, and this is a matter of national security, do *you* want to be the one who let her get away?'

'We might as well, I suppose,' said the man with the theatre tickets. 'This is the first time all holiday my two have agreed on anything. That's a miracle, in my books.'

'This *is* more exciting than the London Eye,' admitted the woman from Florida eagerly.

The captain tried to protest again, but by this time the whole crowd – led by the children – had turned against him. He grumbled under his breath as he returned to his cabin.

Moments later, the boat's speed picked up, eliciting

a cheer from the now frenzied passengers. 'Hold on to your hats!' shouted Frankie, with a punch to the air. Meanwhile Olive was shielding her eyes, trying to spot the red boat along the river. Though they were getting closer, Agent Nest was still far away.

For a moment, as they zipped over the water, Olive was hopeful that they'd be able to close the distance. But soon her hope faded. 'We're just not fast enough,' Olive cried, deflated. 'We'll never catch up at this rate.'

*We need another plan* . . . she thought. *But what?*

Olive searched her brain desperately for a solution. Frankie, meanwhile, was staring out at all the boats moving up and down the river. 'I've got an idea!' he cried suddenly. At first, he was so excited he couldn't get his words out. Then, calming down, he explained. 'The river is a bit like a chess board. We can use the other boats like pieces to block off the queen.'

Olive didn't understand at first. 'A chess board . . . ?' Then it hit her. 'Block the queen. Oh! You're brilliant!' It was another preposterous idea, but it might just work.

Frankie blushed. 'Go, go!' he urged, and Olive turned on her heel and rushed to the captain's office.

'The boat can't go any faster,' he said defensively as Olive opened her mouth to speak.

'No, I know,' she replied. 'That's why we need to put out a message to all the boats in the area that we need their help.'

'We can't just . . .' the captain began, then he stopped and shook his head. 'I thought that nothing else could surprise me on this job. But now here we are, on a high-speed chase to catch spies.' The captain shrugged and handed her the radio. 'Knock yourself out, kid.'

Olive held the radio in her hand, trembling.

'Attention to all vessels on the River Thames. This is Olive Jones with an urgent message. There's a red speedboat approaching . . .' Olive trailed off, realising she didn't know the name of the huge bridge up ahead. She looked to the captain, who mouthed the words *Tower Bridge* at her. Olive went on: 'There's a red speedboat approaching Tower Bridge, coming from a –' the captain mouthed the word *westerly* at her – 'from a westerly direction. The driver of the red boat is highly dangerous and needs to be placed in police custody. If you're in the area, do not let that red boat pass! Form a blockage if you can. The boat must be stopped!'

Olive replaced the radio and returned to the deck. She took a deep breath.

'Did you put out a call?' asked Frankie as she returned. 'Do you think they'll listen?'

'We're about to find out.' Olive shaded her eyes as she scanned the river ahead. *Please let this work*, she thought, *please, please*.

At first it didn't look like anything was happening. Boats were sailing along the river just as they had before. It wasn't until they were nearly at Tower Bridge that Olive saw it – a line of small boats was sitting just after the bridge, one next to the other, so there was no room to pass. Beyond the line of boats, even more were on their way, forming a huge congestion of ships and barges, tourist boats and dinghies. And in front, between the City Sights Cruise boat and the blockade, was the little red speedboat. Olive and Frankie gave great howls of victory and the whole boat erupted into cheers.

The captain hooted the horn as they pulled close to the red boat. Olive ran to the cabin and the captain handed her a loudspeaker. 'Hand yourself in, Agent Natasha Nest!' Olive's voice rang out. 'There's nowhere left to go.'

On the red speedboat, Agent Nest looked furiously up at the tourist boat. The tourists were pressed to the side of the boat staring down at her. Above, people on the bridge had stopped to watch the commotion too, holding out phones to take photos and videos. A helicopter whirred above. Police officers rushed down the riverbank on either side. Agent Nest gave an anguished cry. She was trapped. And she knew it.

The helicopter was now hovering over the small red boat. Olive thought it must be Howard and her grandmother coming to help, or perhaps even the police. But then, with a sickening lurch of her belly, she saw Agent Nest's face morph into a look of triumph. And Olive realised exactly who it must be in the helicopter above. That second a ladder dropped through a hatch in the helicopter's belly, descending towards Agent Nest's boat.

'No!' shouted Olive. 'Antoine has come for her. She's going to get away again!'

Agent Nest stared upwards, waiting for the ladder to reach her. Olive's frantic mind searched for a solution. There was nothing she could do to stop the helicopter. As soon as the ladder reached Agent Nest, it was game over. She and Antoine would fly away with the Memoriser – that held their grandmother's original, undoctored memories and the evidence that Agent Nest was Shadow. They would make lots of money showing Professor Thorn's invention to other countries. And neither she nor Antoine would ever face justice. There was only one thing for it. She had to stop Agent Nest from getting hold of the ladder. She had to stop her from entering the helicopter. But it was impossible to do that from the City Sights Cruise. Somehow, she had to board the red boat.

Olive ran over to the captain, who like everyone else was peering up at the hovering helicopter.

'Captain,' she said, 'can you get us closer to the red boat? As close as you possibly can?'

He narrowed his eyes. 'The helicopter up there won't make it easy,' he replied thoughtfully. 'Makes the water choppy. Could crash if I'm not careful.' He considered it a moment longer. Olive sensed he was keen for the challenge but weighing up the damage it might do to the boat and the trouble he'd be in. 'Could go wrong . . . but I think I can manage the risks,' he said finally, before turning back towards the cabin with the excited air of someone who had driven up and down the same river for years and was finally allowed to have a little fun.

'Erm . . . what are you doing?' asked Frankie cautiously, once the captain was out of earshot.

'I'm going to jump.' Leaning over the edge and staring down at the water below, Olive sized up the distance between the boats. She knew she could make it, if only they got a bit closer. 'If I don't do this, she'll get away with everything – and I can't let that happen!'

Olive felt the engine start back up and the boat begin to move. As it edged closer towards the red boat, Olive considered what she was planning to do. She wasn't stupid; she knew exactly how dangerous it was. If she didn't jump far enough, she'd land in the freezing water below. She might even get caught between the two boats in the process. But if she wanted to stop Agent Nest getting away with the Memoriser – getting away with everything she'd done – it was her only option.

On the red boat, Agent Nest was looking over at Olive and laughing. 'Give up!' she yelled across the water, straining her voice over the noise of the helicopter above. 'Can't you see that it's over?'

This only made Olive feel even more determined. That moment, the captain leaned out from the cabin and signalled with a thumbs up that they were as close as they could get. There was still at least two arm's lengths between the boats. Olive had jumped farther than that before, but never with such high stakes.

Walking through the crowd of passengers, who were busily taking videos of the helicopter, she took the steps down to the lower deck, walking along the side of the boat until she was in the best position she could manage for the jump.

Frankie followed behind fretfully. 'Are you sure you want to do this?' he called. 'What if you don't make it?'

Leaning against the railing at the side of boat, Olive swallowed hard. 'I'm sure!' she shouted back.

Then, with a deep breath, she climbed shakily up and over the railing. Frankie held on to her arms from behind to keep her steady. The blades of the helicopter whirred noisily above. Agent Nest was too busy staring upwards at the lowering ladder to realise what Olive was about to attempt.

'This is it,' she shouted to her brother. 'It's now or never.'

'OK . . . after three, jump,' shouted Frankie. 'Are you ready? One . . . two . . .'

As soon as Olive heard 'three', she launched herself from the boat, as high and as far as she could. She flew through the air for what seemed like an eternity, the cold dark water spreading out beneath her, and she hoped with all her might that she had jumped far enough.

# CHAPTER EIGHTEEN

## Making Memories

With a bruising thump, Olive hit the deck of Agent Nest's boat. She knew instantly that damage had been done, probably to her shoulder, definitely to her knees. But in that moment, she didn't care. The adrenaline pumping through her body kept her from feeling the full impact of her injuries. That would come later. Now she just felt the overwhelming relief at having, somehow, landed the jump safely.

She was only distantly aware of cheers coming from City Sights Cruise as she launched herself at Agent Nest.

But the agent was ready for her and moved away in time. There was a wild look in her eye as she stood over Olive, triumphant. She took something from her pocket – it was the Memoriser. 'Is this what you're after?' She laughed. 'You're good, Olive, but you're no match for a trained agent.' Olive let out a cry of anguish. She'd managed to survive the jump only to allow the Memoriser to slip through her fingers – again.

*No*, she thought. *Not this time.*

It took Olive only a second to decide what to do. She threw herself forwards again, but this time at the boat's steering wheel, grabbing it and pulling it as hard as she could to one side. At the same time, she shoved forward the accelerator. The suddenness of the boat's movement took Agent Nest by surprise. She staggered, losing her balance, and the Memoriser flew out of her hands, soaring through the air, right over the side of the boat and down into the water beneath. Olive pulled the steering wheel back to the centre, and the boat steadied, bobbing in the choppy water.

'No!' Agent Nest screamed, rushing to the side of the boat. She stared aghast at the murky water below. The Memoriser was already halfway to the riverbed. Agent Nest's chance of selling the technology to other countries was gone. As were Grandma Sylvie's memories.

Agent Nest gave a low growl of fury. Then, narrowing her eyes, she turned away from Olive, reaching for where, moments before, the bottom of the ladder had been hanging. But her fingertips clasped only air. Looking upwards, Olive saw the rope being reeled upwards through the air and back into the helicopter.

'Antoine,' Agent Nest cried to the air above. 'Antoine, what are you doing? You can't leave me!'

Olive knew then that Antoine had given up on her. He had no interest in helping her without the Memoriser to sell. There was, after all, no honour among thieves.

In no time at all, the rope had coiled all the way up. Agent Natasha Nest gave a cry of anguish before slumping down on to the seat, head in her hands. Olive caught a final glimpse of Antoine Levigne before the helicopter veered away across the London skyline.

'It's over, Shadow,' said Olive. She looked back to City Sights Cruise, and to Frankie, who was whooping with his fist in the air. She gave him a wave to signal everything was OK. And finally, it was.

\*

It was the longest – and in fact only – hug that Olive remembered receiving from her grandmother. She didn't even try to stop her tears wetting her grandmother's blouse. After a moment though, Olive pulled away. She felt her grandmother's arms loosen, and Olive took a small step backwards, looking up into Grandma Sylvie's steady brown eyes. They were standing on the road by the river where her grandmother (and a small army of police officers) had been waiting for them when Agent Nest finally admitted defeat and turned herself in.

'That was quite the jump,' said her grandmother, handing Olive a handkerchief. 'Your landing could have done with some work, but I can't fault your bravery.' She turned to Frankie, who was standing a little way away. 'And very fine work from you too, young man. Particularly on that evidence you uncovered.'

'Thanks,' said Olive quietly. She wasn't quite sure what to say or how to feel. She wanted to accept her grandmother's praise. She knew she should be happy that Grandma Sylvie was there, alive and well, and of course she *was*. But at the same time, Olive couldn't help but feel hurt. Hurt that their grandmother had lied to them. That she had tricked them. That she hadn't trusted them with her most important secret of all.

'You . . . you let us believe you were dead.' Olive's voice was small and fragile. All the emotion she'd kept down over the previous few weeks was finally bubbling to the surface.

Grandma Sylvie placed her hands gently on her grandchildren's shoulders. 'I'm truly sorry for deceiving you. Believe me, I didn't do so lightly, Olive, but I had thought about it for a long time and I came to the conclusion that faking my death was the only way to draw Shadow out into the light.'

Olive stared at her shoes. 'Why couldn't you have just told us about your plan? We wouldn't have told a soul.'

Grandma Sylvie shook her head. 'I know you wouldn't have, Olive. But doing so would have put your lives at terrible risk.'

'But you *did* put our lives at terrible risk!' said Frankie. To Olive's surprise, he sounded not just hurt, but angry too. It was good to know she wasn't the only one struggling to come to terms with what their grandmother had done. 'As soon as you left us the Memoriser, we were in danger.'

Grandma Sylvie sighed. 'I know it may not seem like it, Frankie, but I was watching over you carefully from afar,' she replied, 'to make sure no harm came to you. I was quite sure, though, that with all the clues I'd left you, with my car, with the gadgets and the watch – and most importantly, with each other – you two would be quite capable of looking after yourselves, and *maybe* even of solving the mission at the same time.' Grandma Sylvie smiled up at them both. 'And I was right.'

Olive and Frankie shared a look. Olive tried hard not to smile. She wasn't ready to let Grandma Sylvie off the hook yet.

'One thing I don't understand,' said Olive, 'why *did* you leave your memories with Professor Thorn, if you didn't trust him?'

'I'd been growing suspicious of Forget Me Not for some time. Something about the company didn't seem right, like how Lachlan Thorn was managing to fund such eye-wateringly expensive research. I was sure that he was working with Shadow, that it was the selling of *my* secrets that was funding his research. Then I heard about the possible partnership between Forget Me Not and the British Intelligence Service and I knew I *had* to make a move. My hope was that having my memories recorded then faking my own death would embolden Shadow and Professor Thorn to act. Of course, I didn't know *how* exactly, but as it turned out, it worked a treat.'

Olive thought back to her first meeting with

Ms Lowry in Grandma Sylvie's bungalow. She'd had no idea then of the adventure – and the danger – that lay ahead.

'But why did you leave Ms Lowry in charge?' Olive asked, her forehead furrowed.

'I didn't like trusting Ms Lowry,' began Grandma Sylvie. 'But I had to ask somebody to tell you about the Memoriser and make the necessary arrangements, and in the end, she played her part well enough. Of course, she told Howard Sweet about the Memoriser, which she shouldn't have. A slip of the tongue I expect. And, as you know, he went straight away to steal it from you. So foolish . . . so hot-headed.' Her lips were pursed disapprovingly.

'Her office was a total mess when we went to see her,' said Frankie, 'like she'd gone into hiding.'

'Ms Lowry was being closely investigated by the British Intelligence Service after Shadow – or Agent Nest – framed her as my accomplice. To escape being arrested, she decided to disappear for a while. A good thing too, or she would have come into trouble. I discovered she's hiding out in a villa in the south of Spain, enjoying the first holiday she's had in years. She's very impressed with you two, by the way.'

'We found Ms Lowry's diary,' said Frankie, 'but

then we handed it straight to Agent Nest. She must have been worried that Howard would figure out she was the one framing you, Grandma. And that if we found him, he'd tell us too. That's why she took the diary.'

'Not the only thing she's ever stolen, as it turns out.' Grandma Sylvie shook her head sadly. 'What a shame it is to have an old friend betray you. Violet Nest's death was tragic. I honestly tried everything to stop her going to the meeting that day, but she wouldn't listen. I'd often got the sense she thought I was jealous of her . . . total nonsense. As a true friend should, I cheered on her many accomplishments. When she couldn't accept the responsibility for her actions, however, she blamed me instead. Agent Nest isn't a bad person. But her grief led her to do terrible things. She took out her pain, her anger, not just on me but on the whole world.'

'What will happen to her?' asked Frankie. Olive could tell that, even after everything she'd done, Frankie still didn't like to think of her suffering.

Grandma Sylvie put a hand on his shoulder. 'I expect she'll go to prison for a very long time.'

'Why did you think Howard might be Shadow?' Frankie asked suddenly. 'He's so nice.'

Grandma Sylvie sighed. 'I certainly did have my suspicions about Howard, to my shame. It's hard to know who to trust when there's a mole around. And Howard and I have had more than a few arguments over the years. But I was wrong to doubt him.'

Now Olive understood her grandmother's plans, her feelings of betrayal faded. For the second time in her life, she swung her arms around her grandmother. 'Grandma Sylvie, I'm so glad you're safe.'

'I'm proud of you both.' Grandma Sylvie gradually loosened her grip. 'Agent Nest could have done untold damage if her plan had gone ahead. She could have changed memories whenever it suited her. Edited out information she didn't want agents to remember. Added events that had never happened. That kind of power . . . ? It was unthinkable.'

Their heads turned towards Agent Nest, who that moment was being walked, handcuffed, towards a police car. She ducked as she was guided inside. Olive just caught a glimpse of Professor Thorn, who was already sitting in the car, before the door was slammed shut.

Olive and Frankie watched thoughtfully as the police car carrying Agent Nest and Professor Thorn drove down the street and disappeared around a corner. They were so busy watching the car that at first, they didn't notice when someone appeared behind them.

'I don't believe my eyes,' the person said. They turned in unison.

Howard Sweet was taking a handkerchief from the pocket of his brown leather bomber jacket and dabbing at his temples. 'Sylvie Jones . . . you're not . . . you're . . .'

'Hello, Howard.' She smiled again – the second smile either of the children had ever seen their grandmother give. 'Yes, I am.'

'I knew you couldn't be . . .' he faltered. 'I knew you had to be alive.'

'First things first.' Grandma Sylvie spoke stiffly. Her face was proud, her eyes looking up at the sky. 'I'm sure by now you'll know I had a dossier on you. I'm sorry that I thought it possible you were a mole, Howard. I hope we can be friends again . . . or enemies . . . or whatever we are this week. I've rather missed beating you at chess.'

Howard Sweet glared at her for a moment, then his hunched shoulders relaxed. 'All's fair in love and war, as they say, Sylvie.' Looking down at Olive and Frankie, his eyes brightened. 'And I must admit, you have quite the pair of grandchildren.'

'At least we can agree on that,' said Grandma Sylvie with a nod.

Olive smiled. Grandma Sylvie was still the grandmother they'd always known, not one to waste words. But underneath her hard shell, Olive now knew she cared deeply for her grandchildren.

'I missed most of the action, it seems,' said Howard gloomily. 'I tried to break into the meeting to help, but MI6 security were sniffing around. I knew that if one of the guards had recognised me they would have realised something was up. So, I decided to make myself useful and pick up a certain somebody instead . . .'

The next moment, Olive and Frankie heard a familiar voice calling from somewhere behind.

'You're OK! Are you hurt?'

They turned and were astonished to see their mother rushing across the bridge towards them. Her face was drawn and puffy with worry. When she reached them, she swept her two children up into her arms in one go.

'We're fine!' they both replied in chorus.

'What on earth is going on?' As usual their mother had a remarkable ability to flit between concern and anger at an unsettling speed. 'Do you have any idea how much trouble you two are in?'

Frankie looked at his shoes. 'Sorry, Mum. But we were doing something important, promise!'

'I know exactly what you were doing. Somebody took a live video of the whole thing and put it on the internet. It's gone viral! I thought, those two children look familiar, but it can't possibly be *my* children, because they're safely at school . . .' She gave them a piercing look. 'Next thing I knew, a *helicopter* landed in the garden to pick me up.'

'We were here to help Grandma Sylvie,' said Olive, stepping aside to reveal her grandmother. She hoped that the revelation that Grandma Sylvie was alive might be enough to distract her mother from her anger – at least for a minute.

'Oh, yes. Hello, Sylvie,' said their mother as if it were the most normal thing in the world. Then the realisation hit. 'Sylvie!' Her eyes were wide. 'You're alive! Oh, I should have known . . .' she said, laughing.

Grandma Sylvie smiled. 'Good afternoon, Helen.'

Olive was taken aback. 'Umm . . . Mum, what exactly do you mean, *you should have known*? Aren't you a bit more *surprised*? Grandma was supposed to be . . . er . . . dead.'

'Oh, yes. Well, I wouldn't put anything past your grandmother.' She looked down at her children, who were frowning up at her. 'Let's just say I may have known a little more about her life than perhaps you two did – though by the sounds of it you're up to speed now.' Their mother ignored the shocked expressions on Olive and Frankie's faces. 'Which means I guess it's probably time I tell you about your father too . . .'

Olive and Frankie looked at each other, their eyes wide.

'About Dad?' Olive squeaked. She didn't think she could take more family secrets.

'Is Dad a spy too?' whispered Frankie.

'Well let's just say, it does rather seem to run in the family,' said Grandma Sylvie with a wink at her grandchildren.

'We'll get into that later,' said Mum firmly, 'after we finish discussing your *year-long punishment*.'

There was a polite cough, and Olive looked up to see Sir Bobbie Eden strolling towards them with his chest puffed out and arms tucked behind his back.

'Sorry to interrupt this little reunion. I just wanted to say a very well done to our two young operatives here,' he said, smiling down at Olive and Frankie.

'The British Intelligence Service owes you two a big thank you. It would have been rather . . . embarrassing . . . to have allowed such a catastrophic security breach take place under my watch. When you two turn eighteen, give me a call. I can see a career in this business in your futures.'

As he walked away, Olive and Frankie shared a look of astonishment. Then, suddenly, Frankie's face fell.

'What is it?' asked Olive.

'I just remembered that we won't get to see Grandma's memories now.'

'Ahem,' said Grandma Sylvie from behind Frankie's back. 'You won't *need* my memories any more. You'll have *me*.'

'But what if it all goes back to like it was before, and we hardly ever see you? What if nothing changes?' asked Frankie.

'Believe me, I never liked being so cold and distant from you. But with Shadow in my life, I knew I had to. In order to protect you both.'

Olive was reminded of one of the memories she'd seen at Forget Me Not. 'That day when Shadow broke into your house . . . you were with me in my pram.'

'That was the last straw. I knew I couldn't put you

in danger like that again. From that day I vowed to keep my distance. I hoped that when you watched my memories, you'd finally understand why. I also hoped the memories from my school days might encourage you to believe in yourself a little more, Olive. To show that you aren't the only one who finds herself in trouble, despite her best intentions.'

Hearing this, Olive's face lit up. Looking at Grandma Sylvie, she saw her for a moment as the young girl in her headteacher's office about to be expelled, the girl with an uncertain future, who would grow up to be the legendary Sylvie Jones – spy, mother, grandmother. Unable to put her emotions into words, Olive simply smiled.

Frankie, meanwhile, had brightened. 'So now Shadow is gone, everything can change? You won't need to stay away any more?'

'There are always dangers in my career, and I'm afraid I do travel a lot. But yes, I think we can spend much more time together than we ever did before. And I'm going to start taking things a little easier too, taking some time off here and there. As for the memories, lucky for you two I have them all locked up here.' She tapped her temple. 'All you have to do is ask.'

As the group made their way across the bridge, to

start their journey home again, Howard Sweet leaned over to Olive and Frankie. 'I've got a few memories I could share about that grandmother of yours too. Tell me, you two,' he said conspiratorially, 'have you ever heard about the time your grandmother and I parachuted into Buenos Aires? No, I didn't think so. Well, we were sitting in the plane, ready to do the jump. When I turned to Sylvie, and I said . . .'

*

In the days that followed, the video footage of the children's adventure on the Thames vanished without a trace before any of their classmates or teachers could see it. There was no mention in any of the newspapers or television news programmes about what had happened either. As far as everyone knew at school, both Olive and Frankie had got chicken pox and spent the day itching and watching cartoons on daytime television.

Grandma Sylvie returned to her bungalow and her beloved cat James, who greeted her with a swish of his ginger tail which suggested that all along he'd known she hadn't gone far. Though he retained his air of wildness, the cat became friendlier with the

287

children over the weeks that followed and soon Frankie came to consider James his own pet as much as his grandmother's. Some things didn't change: Grandma Sylvie was still prone to disappear for days, weeks, and sometimes even months at a time. But whenever she was at home, the lace curtains of her cottage were kept open – a signal for Olive and Frankie that they were welcome to come over.

On Sunday evenings in particular, the pair often went to Grandma Sylvie's after dinner. They'd sit in the armchairs in her secret basement. Frankie and Grandma would play chess while Olive would ask questions about how Grandma became a spy, her most dangerous missions and most hair-raising escapes. Lots and lots and lots of questions. Most of the questions their grandmother would answer happily, some she would simply pretend not to hear. Then, when she'd had enough, she would give a wide yawn and suggest the children had better go home to bed.

As soon as she got home after these evenings, Olive would make detailed notes of her grandmother's best stories in a little notebook she kept safely under her pillow. Often the notes from an evening would run over pages and pages. She would write until her wrist ached and her eyes grew heavy. Sometimes these stories would inspire Olive to write her own stories, which she would stay up late into the night crafting. Her stories would often start with the truth – a detail her grandmother had shared, like an exotic location or a mission that had gone disastrously wrong – and then Olive would let her imagination take the reins. She considered the little notebook the most treasured possession she had. Second only, perhaps, to her imagination itself.

Besides this, Olive returned to her ordinary life, getting into trouble at school, not listening when she should, getting carried away with her over-active imagination. Life was just as it had been before. She longed to tell people the truth about her incredible Grandma Sylvie. But she knew she couldn't. And nobody would have believed her even if she had. Instead, when people asked her about her family, Olive would smile and say that they were entirely, perfectly ordinary. Certainly not the kind of family who had secrets. What you saw was what you got. And Olive wouldn't have changed them for the world.

# ACKNOWLEDGEMENTS

If you ask me, the process of writing a book is a lot like completing a jigsaw puzzle. As soon as the puzzle is finished, you step back, look at the completed picture, and wonder why it took you so long to get there.

Along the way, though, the task feels impossible. You start to suspect that pieces are missing from the box. You try to stuff pieces in where they don't fit. You have to take apart big sections to start all over again. Then, gradually, you discover the right outline. You find a missing corner piece that's been hiding under the rug. And over time the puzzle begins to take shape. Eventually, you find the book you set out to write.

That's the experience I've had with this book. It's been both challenging and enormously fun. And there are lots of people I'd like to thank for helping along the way.

Firstly, thank you to my brilliant and creative editor, Lena McCauley. Without your insights the puzzle pieces would have forever been in the wrong places. Thank you for being so patient along the way and for making the book a million times better than it would have been otherwise. Thank you also to the book's copyeditor, Lily Morgan, for her superb notes and razor-sharp edits.

My sincere thanks once again go to Michelle Brackenborough, who designed the cover, and to Thy Bui, who created the cover illustration. Thank you to the whole team at Hachette, including the book's publicist, Lucy Clayton, and marketer, Bec Gillies, and everyone in production, sales, rights, distribution and beyond.

Thank you to my amazing agent, Chloe Seager, for your support throughout the writing process and for your guidance and wisdom. Thanks also to Vanessa at Madeline Milburn for sharing your valuable feedback on an early draft.

Thank you to my wonderful colleagues at Penguin, especially Thi Dinh for being so supportive. Thanks also to Rosie Glaisher, who was hugely encouraging when I told her about my first book and has been ever since.

Thank you to my amazing friends. Over the years you've taught me lots about what friendship means, which has been very helpful when writing about it for children. Thanks also to my new friends from the Good Ship 2021 group, who over the last year have been a support I've hugely valued.

A massive thanks go to Mum, Dad and Jo. You're the best first readers I could ever ask for. Thank you for examining every draft so forensically and for always championing everything I do. Huge thanks also to Cerys, Gill, Gary, and the Budges for their support, and to the rest of my family.

Thank you to Andrew. You've been with me every step of the way. Literally sitting a few metres away lots of the time, as this book was mostly written in lockdown. On our daily walks we talked through everything from the characters to the plot, and you showed endless patience and kindness. No matter what, you never let me give up. There would be no book without you.

Finally, I'd like to thank booksellers, librarians and teachers who work so hard to bring stories to children. There would be no readers without you.

## HAVE YOU EVER THOUGHT WHAT IT MIGHT BE LIKE IF YOU WERE FAMOUS IN THE FUTURE?

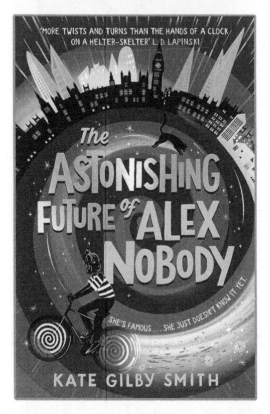

On the day Alex was born, crowds surrounded the hospital. On her first day of school, people spied from the gates. And recently, strangers came to watch her perform in the school play . . . as the llama.

But why? Alex has always been a nobody.

Then a mysterious boy named Jasper starts at school and he alone seems to know the answer. But before he can tell Alex, he disappears . . . into the future. Can Alex brave travelling into the futre to unravel the secret of her astonishing destiny . . . before time runs out?

# KATE GILBY SMITH

was born on the sunny island of Guernsey.
It was daydreaming during a philosophy of
time travel seminar at Edinburgh University
that she first had the idea for her first book,
*The Astonishing Future of Alex Nobody*.
Alongside being an author, she works as a
publicist at a London publisher of science,
philosophy and history books.

 @kate_gilby